Dear Valentine,

I've been waiting for so long to tell you how I feel, and now I can't find the right words. You are the most amazing girl I've ever known, and no one else has ever measured up. Maybe our relationship is in the past, but I hope it can still have a future too.

It's still coming out wrong. So why don't you let me say it in person?

Meet me at First and Ten tonight at 6 P.M. I'll be carrying a red rose.

Don't miss any of the books in SWEET VALLEY HIGH
SENIOR YEAR, an exciting series from Bantam Books!

Visit the Official Sweet Valley Web Site on the Internet at:

www.sweetvalley.com

Francine Pascal's SVH senioryear

Be Mine

CREATED BY
FRANCINE PASCAL

BANTAM BOOKS
NEW YORK · TORONTO · LONDON · SYDNEY · AUCKLAND

RL: 6, AGES 012 AND UP

BE MINE

A Bantam Book / January 2002

Sweet Valley High® is a registered trademark of Francine Pascal.
Conceived by Francine Pascal.
Cover photography by Michael Segal.

Copyright © 2002 by Francine Pascal.
Cover copyright © 2002 by 17th Street Productions,
an Alloy, Inc. company.

Produced by 17th Street Productions,
an Alloy, Inc. company.
151 West 26th Street
New York, NY 10011.

ISBN: 0-553-49386-8

Visit us on the Web! www.randomhouse.com/teens

Published simultaneously in the United States and Canada

Bantam Books is an imprint of Random House Children's Books, a
division of Random House, Inc. BANTAM BOOKS and the rooster
colophon are registered trademarks of Random House, Inc. Bantam Books,
1540 Broadway, New York, New York 10036.

PRINTED IN THE UNITED STATES OF AMERICA

OPM   0 9 8 7 6 5 4 3 2 1

To Debbie Jacobs & John Lee

TIA RAMIREZ

IS IT REALLY VALENTINE'S DAY ALREADY? PERFECT TIMING. WHY COULDN'T IT HAVE BEEN IN THE FALL, BACK WHEN I <u>HAD</u> A BOYFRIEND? I JUST NEED TO KEEP REMINDING MYSELF THAT IT'S BETTER TO BE ALONE THAN TO BE WITH SOMEONE WHO DOESN'T DESERVE ME. SOMEONE WHO WOULD ACTUALLY HIT ON ONE OF MY FRIENDS, EVEN IF HE'S SPENT EVERY MINUTE SINCE TRYING TO CONVINCE ME IT WAS A MISTAKE. I CAN GET THROUGH THIS. IT'S JUST ONE DAY, RIGHT?

Andy Marsden

Valentine's Day couldn't be coming at a worse time this year. I mean, it's never been my favorite holiday. But this year is the first V-day when I should be able to be happy. I finally met someone I really like, and he even likes me too. I never understood when Tia tried to explain how "complicated" relationships could be, how even when you both care about each other, it doesn't always work. I thought she was just a drama queen. Maria and Liz too. But now I get it. Just in time for the day of love.

Elizabeth Wakefield

Okay, it's Valentine's Day. Fine. Why should that bother me? Yeah, this time last year I was perfectly happy with Todd, convinced we'd be together forever. And now he's dating the younger sister of my ex-boyfriend, the younger sister of the guy I can't seem to find a way to get over for good. No big deal, right? I can handle being single. I can handle not having a valentine.

I really need a boyfriend.

Jade Wu

I'm so psyched that it's finally Valentine's Day! I've never actually had a boyfriend on Valentine's Day before. Well, I guess I never really had boyfriends, period. But everything's different with me and Evan. I know he's going to do something special for me—that's just Evan. And I can't wait to see what it is. . . .

CHAPTER

HAPPY COUPLELAND

1

Evan Plummer blinked open his eyes and rolled over onto his side to look at the clock on his bedside table. Bright sunshine streamed in through the drapes on his window, and he had to squint to read the time. Six forty-five. For once he wouldn't have to rush. He had plenty of time to make the bell. He could even grab some breakfast before his shower.

He stretched his arms over his head and stared up at the ceiling, running a hand through his grubby hair as he tried to wake up.

He had slept with his window open and had to smile as he glanced out at the sunlight. Only in southern California could he sleep with his window open in the middle of February.

Then suddenly his smile disappeared as he realized what today was. February 14—Valentine's Day. And to think he'd almost been in a good mood for the first time since his parents had told him they were getting a divorce. But now he would be bombarded with hearts, flowers, love, and cards all day. Happy smiling couples were not what he needed to see right now. Even though he had Jade, and he was definitely happy with her, he just wasn't up for facing a day celebrating relationships when his parents were splitting up.

Evan groaned, his body feeling like lead. The last thing he wanted to do was get up and go to school. But there was really no other way out. He had a quiz in Spanish, so playing sick wasn't an option.

Time to face the music, Plummer, he thought as he threw back the sheet. *Move one foot in front of the other and get through this day.* He made his way to the bathroom down the hall and squeezed toothpaste onto his toothbrush.

As he brushed, Evan caught his reflection in the mirror. The frown on his face was probably going to be there all day. He hoped Jade wasn't expecting him to make a big deal out of Valentine's Day. He hadn't even been able to force himself to look at the rows of lovey-dovey cards at the mall, let alone buy her candy or flowers or anything. But luckily Jade wasn't one of those girls who got into that stuff. That was one of the things he liked so much about her—she could be happy with simple pleasures, like he was.

Evan rinsed off his toothbrush and turned off the bathroom light. As he stepped into the hall, he

2

smelled toast and coffee coming from downstairs. His mom was up, which meant he could just have some of whatever she'd made for breakfast. Evan took the stairs slowly, staring at the pictures of him, his mom, and his dad that lined the walls of the stairway. They started at the top of the stairs with the oldest family portrait, when Evan was just a baby, and went down through the years to the most recent, taken just a couple of months ago at Christmas. He tried to see a change in his mom's or dad's faces, looking for a forced expression or some clue of what had been wrong. But they looked so happy in each one, especially the most recent. Who would have guessed his mom was in love with another guy? Evan shook his head.

The Plummers' kitchen was even brighter and sunnier than Evan's bedroom had been, and Evan had to blink to see his mom standing next to the counter. But he heard her right away. She was humming while she buttered her cinnamon-raisin toast, clearly not aware that he was standing there. Evan cleared his throat.

"Oh, good morning, honey!" Mrs. Plummer said, giving him a quick, awkward glance. "You're up early today." She turned from Evan right away and returned her gaze to the counter, intently cutting her toast. No more humming, though. "There's toast and cereal, and you know the juice is in the fridge. . . . ," she said, her voice higher-pitched than usual.

"Mom, it's okay," Evan said as he opened the refrigerator and took out the orange juice. "You don't have to apologize for being happy. You can keep humming if you want." He slammed the refrigerator door a little too hard, then winced.

His mom walked toward the table to sit down. Evan got a bowl and filled it with cereal and milk, then sighed and sat down across from her. The awkward silences had been killing him lately. He just wanted to finish his cereal and hit the shower. The sooner this day started, the sooner it could end.

"So, do you have plans with Jade tonight?" Mrs. Plummer asked. She was still avoiding looking at Evan and instead stared at her coffee cup as she spoke.

"Nah," Evan said with a shrug. "I'll probably hang out with the guys."

"Well, I—I have a date tonight," she said cautiously, taking a long sip of coffee. Evan caught her glance at him over the top of her cup. Even though Evan knew his mom was worried about how everything was affecting him—the separation, his dad moving out, her new boyfriend—she still had that Valentine's glow around her. Her cheeks were flushed, and her eyes were bright. Evan knew he

4

should be happy for her, but there was no way. Not now. He felt the corners of his mouth turn down, and he shifted in the wooden kitchen chair.

Mrs. Plummer caught his expression, and her smile sagged. "I can cancel if it upsets you, Evan," she said, looking at him directly for the first time since he came downstairs. "I know this must be hard for you."

Evan felt his chest tighten as he shoveled another spoonful of cereal into his mouth. Of course he didn't want her to see Mr. Niles, but if they didn't go out tonight, they'd be on a date the next night, so what was the point in him objecting?

"Don't bother canceling," he said. "I probably won't be around anyway, remember?"

"Okay," Mrs. Plummer breathed, looking a little relieved. She took her plate and mug to the sink and ran the water. "Are you sure Jade is okay with not celebrating Valentine's Day?" she asked.

"Yeah, she's not into that stuff," Evan replied. "I just want to chill out tonight anyway."

He pushed his chair back from the table, and Mrs. Plummer took his bowl and glass. "Thanks, Mom," he said as he headed for the stairs.

"Well, if I don't see you, have a good time tonight," she said loudly as he walked away.

"Yeah, uh, you too." Evan could barely choke out

the words. He didn't turn around because his face would give away that what he just said wasn't true. He didn't want his mom and Mr. Niles to have a good time. He really wanted Mr. Niles to move to Alaska and never see his mom again. A knot formed in his neck as he took the stairs two at a time.

Hopefully he'd be able to hang out with Andy and Conner later. They would be as happy as he was to let this holiday pass—unnoticed.

"Whoa! Where am I?" Tia asked Andy as they walked in the front door of Sweet Valley High.

"I don't think we're in Kansas anymore," Andy joked, looking at the pink and red streamers and balloons lining the hallways.

SVH had been transformed overnight into valentine central. Cutout cupids and hearts were pasted on the walls, and little paper hearts that looked like confetti were scattered on the floor. There was a booth set up in the corner, where student-government reps were selling candygrams. There was no mistaking what day it was.

"Are our school colors red and pink now?" Tia joked back, taking it all in. She felt a pang. The school did look great, and if she were in a relationship right now, she would have been loving the decorations. But since she was painfully single, all they

6

did was remind her of that fact. At least Andy was feeling as cynical as she was.

"This holiday has nothing to do with the school itself," Andy said, lifting his sneaker to brush off a few of the paper hearts stuck to the bottom. "Why are they making such a big deal out of it? El Carro never did anything like this."

"This is Sweet Valley High." Tia shrugged. "They always go overboard with the school spirit. I'm surprised they didn't make a bigger deal out of Groundhog Day."

"Seriously," Andy said.

They walked slowly toward the crowds of students in the center of the hall, chuckling.

But they soon grew quiet. All around them students were hugging and kissing, talking about their plans for that night.

In her three years of high school Tia had never been without a boyfriend on Valentine's Day. This holiday had never seemed depressing until she was on the outside of "happy coupleland" looking in.

And the couples were everywhere! It was like people had paired up overnight. Tia knew she hadn't seen so many smiling people holding hands the day before.

Some kind of conspiracy must be going on here, she thought, looking down at the floor. If there were someplace to hide, she would be there right now. But Tia knew it was only going to get worse as the day went on and students got more and more excited about their valentine dates. She'd never studied her shoes so intently before.

"That's it," Andy said. "Just don't look and maybe they'll all go away. Or let me use you as a shield to block out all the couples," he said, pulling her out in front of him.

Tia had to laugh. But she knew today was bound to bring up feelings of loneliness in Andy. After all, he just came out and finally found a guy he clicked with. But that guy couldn't get up the nerve to tell anyone he was gay. And it wasn't like Sweet Valley was crawling with eligible gay high-school students. If this Valentine's Day was going to be hard on anyone, it was Andy.

"So, what are you doing later?" Tia asked. "Today's not just for couples, you know. It's a day to celebrate your independence and try not to kill any lovebirds in the process." They stopped at the water fountain so that Andy could take a drink.

"Let's see," he said, wiping his mouth on his sleeve. "I have so many dates to choose from, it's mind-boggling, so I'm thinking I'm just gonna leave them all hanging and see if Conner and Evan want to come over and play pool."

"Yeah, I'll probably hang out with Liz or be . . ." Tia trailed off as she watched a giant bouquet of flowers being carried down the hall. *Some guy on his way to surprise his girlfriend,* she thought. He looked so happy, with a huge smile on his face. His girlfriend was going to be tickled pink.

Why did Trent have to have those feelings for Jessica? Everyone wanted her to forget about the fact that he had gone behind her back like that, but Tia just couldn't. She had felt so betrayed.

"Or be what?" Andy prompted.

"Um, what?" Tia snapped back from her thoughts and turned to Andy.

"You said you'll probably hang out with Liz or be . . . what? You never finished what you were saying because you were too busy wishing those flowers were for you."

"Oh, right. No, I don't wish they were for me. But they are pretty."

"Or be what?" Andy asked, not letting her off the hook.

He really wasn't going to let her out of answering. Tia shook her head. "Or be alone," she finished.

Or be alone—that's the alternative she was facing right now. Being alone on Valentine's Day. It couldn't get any worse. As she approached her row of lockers, she saw cards sticking out of the vents,

9

valentines pasted to the fronts. One guy had even gotten creative and wrapped his girlfriend's locker in white wrapping paper and written their names on it with *Forever* written beneath it. It was the kind of stuff that always seemed a little cheesy when you were in a relationship but actually seemed incredibly sweet when you weren't. Tia sighed.

"Well, I'm heading for my locker," Andy said. "Try not to get too depressed today."

"Yeah, you too," Tia said, giving him a supportive smile.

If she could just keep her head down and get through this day, everything would be all right.

Will Simmons pulled his Blazer into the Sweet Valley parking lot, a love song blaring on the radio. It was finally Valentine's Day, and he hadn't been this psyched for the holiday since he and Melissa first got together. So much had happened since then.

Things were different between them now. They were better. They'd been through a lot this year and were still together like they should be. Like they'd always be. Maybe one day—a few years from now—he'd have a ring in his pocket to give Melissa for Valentine's Day.

Will hopped out of his car and grabbed his bag from the backseat. He was actually happy to be in school today. As he walked in the door, he was reminded why. The school looked amazing. It was great how the student council went all out for Valentine's Day, a nonschool-type holiday. Usually they only got this carried away for football games and stuff. The stuff he used to be totally into himself—before the accident.

"Hey, Simmons!" Matt Wells shouted from down the hall. Will turned and waited for Matt to catch up. Matt slapped Will on the back when he reached him. "You have this totally goofy grin on your face, man. I see this Valentine's Day stuff is getting to you too. Seems like every guy I know came to school with flowers today. Jason Henson even brought a big teddy bear through the front door. Poor guy. Glad it wasn't me."

Will smiled. Guys like Matt always made fun of people in relationships, but that was only because he hadn't met the right girl yet. He hadn't met his Melissa.

"So," Matt said. "What are your plans for the big couples' holiday anyway?"

Will grinned. He felt like he'd been planning this night for weeks, and he was psyched at the chance to fill his friend in on everything he was doing. "Well, I'm taking Melissa to this cool restaurant, The Silver Ladle," he began as they headed down the hall

11

together. "Erika suggested we try it. She even told me to request a corner booth. Melissa will be pretty impressed when we get the best table at a trendy, expensive place," Will finished proudly.

"Yeah, you're treating her right. But are you sure you wouldn't rather be taking Erika than Melissa?" Matt teased.

Will felt his face flush red, and he swallowed—hard.

"Hey, I'm kidding," Matt said. "Besides, Erika's on hold for me anyway, right?"

Will tried to regain his cool, but he couldn't help feeling nervous about Matt's comment. He *had* been noticing Erika Brooks a lot at the *Tribune* office lately. But who wouldn't? Erika had been the best-looking senior back at El Carro, and now she was a sophomore in college. It was tough not to check her out. But that didn't mean he didn't want to be with Melissa.

"Sorry, I don't think she'd go for a high-school guy," Will said. Would she?

"I still think I should stop by and visit you at work sometime," Matt said. "Just see what's up there."

"She hasn't changed that much since we knew her," Will said. "I mean, she looks even better, but she still knows just where to go and what to do for everything. She's totally hooked into the SVU world."

"So, is she seeing anyone?" Matt asked, shrugging his backpack higher on his shoulder.

Will frowned. "I don't know," he said. "I don't think so. We hung out after work last Friday, and she took me to some great clubs near SVU. She knew everyone there. We kept running into friends of hers—she's just as popular as she was in high school. But no physical sign of a boyfriend." He paused, shooting a sidelong glance at Matt. "Not that that means anything. For all I know, her boyfriend could have been out of town for the weekend," he added, not really knowing why. He just didn't like the idea of Matt actually trying to go out with her.

"Well, that's no reason to give up. You know, outta sight, outta mind," Matt said, his eyes gleaming. Will laughed, a little too loud.

He was already halfway down the hall before he snapped out of his haze and stopped chuckling. What if Matt was right? Erika was exactly Will's type. Melissa only got annoyed when Will wanted to do well at the *Tribune*, but Erika was just as into the paper. She got it.

Will shook his head. *You're supposed to be focusing on Melissa today, not Erika, Simmons,* he reminded himself. Somehow he'd had to remind himself of that fact a lot lately.

Dear Valentine,

Valentine's Day seemed like ~~a good~~ the perfect time for me to tell you that I'm still thinking about you.

You know who I am, and we have a past, but ~~I'd like to focus on the future~~ I think we should have a future too. (Is that too cheesy?) I ~~think~~ know that we'd be great together. ~~What do you think? I'd like to know what~~ I can't wait to find out what you think. Meet me tonight at First and Ten at 7 P.M. ~~I'll be in the corner booth.~~ I'll have a red rose.

                    Love,
                    Your Secret Admirer

Ugh! Why can't I get this right? It has to be perfect for her. I need to get it right. And fast.

CHAPTER

All Bets Are Off

2

5-31-9. Andy worked the combination on his locker slowly. His problems with Dave had made him pretty depressed, and now Valentine's Day was only making it all ten times worse, reminding him of everything he was missing out on. He sighed and opened his rusty locker door.

Getting through this day was going to be harder than he thought. Harder even than all the others since he broke it off with Dave. Andy knew he'd done the right thing. He'd struggled so much with telling his parents and friends that he was gay, and he just couldn't handle having the first guy he dated force him to keep the relationship a secret. Still, he couldn't help thinking that he'd lost the chance with the only person he'd ever really felt something for.

He grabbed his English-lit book and shoved it in his backpack. Maybe classes could actually help him today by giving him a much needed distraction. Andy surveyed the hall. Of course, Valentine's Day would be even easier if he liked girls. He couldn't help but notice that there wasn't one single same-sex couple at Sweet Valley High. He was the lone token gay guy in a sea of what everyone else saw as totally normal teenage love.

Was the first bell ever going to ring? Where was Tia when he needed her? Off to *her* locker when she should have been sticking to his side.

"Hey, Marsden," a low voice said from behind him.

Andy turned and felt the tension in his shoulders ease as he saw Conner and Evan standing there. Just the guys he wanted to see. These two would definitely be up for ditching the hearts and flowers and hanging out that night. True, they both had girlfriends, but they weren't exactly the sentimental types. Far from it, in fact.

"Can you believe all the decorations?" Evan asked, shaking his head.

"What a waste of funds. They're just gonna have to take it all down tomorrow," Conner agreed. He kicked away some of the confetti on the floor with his work boot.

"Yeah, they went overboard," Andy said as he slammed his locker door shut.

"You know what the problem is? It's this whole Hallmark-holiday thing," Evan said. He leaned

16

against the row of blue lockers and tossed his backpack on the linoleum floor. "Valentine's Day is just an excuse for card companies to make some more money."

"Well, I hope Alanna isn't expecting me to make a fool of myself today 'cause it's not gonna happen," Conner said.

Andy couldn't help smiling at that.

"So instead of toting teddy bears and making declarations of love, let's have a sports challenge," Evan said. "After school okay with you guys?"

"Sounds good," Andy said, relieved. "My basement's open. A little pool, a little Ping-Pong, some darts, and all will be well."

Evan was nodding even before Andy finished talking. "I'd be happy to lock myself in your basement until morning, when all of these decorations are down and things are back to normal. Besides, I've been working on my lethal Ping-Pong serve."

"You needed to work on that," Conner said, giving Evan a push. "But I can't make it. Sorry."

"What's up?" Andy asked, checking his watch to see how much time they had before the first bell.

"I've got plans," Conner said with a shrug.

"Uh-huh," Evan chided. "You've got to do something for Valentine's Day. Admit it."

Conner shifted his weight from one foot to the

other, his eyebrows furrowing together. Andy knew that look. Conner was busted.

"Alanna wants to see this band, Gravity's Daughter, play at The Shack. We're gonna hit it after our A.A. meeting," Conner said.

"Yeah, sure," Andy said, looking over at Evan and winking. "Well, if you change your mind, you know where we'll be. Evan, can you make it over at like five-thirty?"

"Sure," Evan said. "I gotta get to my locker before the bell." He picked up his backpack. I'll see you guys."

"Yeah, see you," Andy said, taking off in the opposite direction down the hall. He actually felt a little better. At least he had a way to pass Valentine's Day now. He and Evan could hide out until February 15—when the world would be normal again.

Tia only had a few minutes to get her books from her locker before homeroom. She'd gotten so distracted wallowing in her misery that she hadn't noticed how fast the time before first period had passed. She'd been watching all the couples a little too intently.

It was really enough to make her want to go straight home. Had every Valentine's Day at Sweet Valley been like this? So festive? So out of control and over the top?

As she turned down to her row of lockers, she saw a note taped to one of the lockers near hers. *Wonderful, another love declaration,* she thought.

But as she got closer, Tia realized that the note was on her locker. Couldn't the person at least get the locker right? She sighed and went to rip off the note, but her breath caught when she saw the name written across the paper. It was for her.

On instinct, she looked around to see if someone was playing a joke on her. She'd kill Andy if he popped out from behind a locker right now and started laughing. But there was no one nearby.

Confused, Tia opened up the note just as Andy rounded the corner.

"Hey, Tee, I got a Valentine's date to hang out with Evan and do nothing. What's that?" he asked, looking at the note in her hand.

"You don't know? It's not a joke from you? A fake valentine?" she asked, raising her eyebrows.

"Negative," he said. "Come on, I'm not that cruel. So who's it from?"

"Uh, I'm not sure." Tia glanced down at the paper. It was on cute valentine stationery with old-fashioned cupids in the corners. The note was typed, so she couldn't tell anything from the handwriting.

"Well, read it. I have exactly two minutes before

I'm late," Andy insisted, his arms crossed in front of his chest.

"Okay," Tia said, her curiosity finally getting the better of her. "'It's Valentine's Day,'" she read aloud. "'A day to forgive and forget and find romance. I'd love another chance with you, Tia. You're worth more than you know to me.'" She scanned for a signature, but there wasn't one. No name.

"It's from Trent," Andy said, smiling. "Cool. He's trying to win back the fair Tia."

"How do you know it's from him? He didn't sign it," Tia said, staring down at the paper.

"Oh, come on, Tia. Trent's been trying to get you back since he pulled that stupid stunt at Jeremy's surprise party."

Tia winced as she recalled that moment she'd overheard Trent talking to Jessica about how the two had "almost kissed." Jessica had straightened her out later and explained that Trent was exaggerating, but she'd still been pretty wrecked over the fact that her boyfriend had even *thought* about kissing one of her best friends.

She shook her head, trying to get rid of that image. She'd made it pretty clear to Trent that she wasn't interested in trying again or starting over. She couldn't have spelled it out any more clearly. But who else did she know who would want another chance with her?

Andy must be right. It was Trent. The guy sure was persistent. Too bad it wasn't going to get him anywhere.

"Well, he can send me as many valentines as he wants, but that won't change anything," Tia said, zipping up her bag.

"Hey, give the guy another chance," Andy said, moving toward her. "It is Valentine's Day, and he does seem sorry."

Tia shrugged. "I just can't forgive it."

"You do get that it's you he wants and not Jessica, right?" Andy pressed. "I mean, he came all the way over here when he goes to school somewhere else just to tape a note on your locker door. That's pretty romantic."

Tia felt a small smile creep across her face, and she bit her lip. Andy was right. It was all pretty romantic, but she didn't want romance right now. She wanted Valentine's Day to be over and all the sentimental stuff to end. Right? Right. Definitely.

I think so.

In frustration she threw the note at Andy and laughed. "I need backup here that this is not the time to forgive old boyfriends," she said. "Weren't you just complaining about this holiday with me over there?"

Andy nodded and picked up the note. "We all make mistakes," he said as he put the note back in

21

her hand. "Gotta run. Bell's gonna ring," he said as he sprinted down the hall.

Tia looked down at the crumpled paper. There was no way she was going to take Trent back. That was final. She was *not* going to be swayed by the Valentine's Day spirit.

Another dude with flowers. Evan nearly chuckled to himself as he walked toward Jade's locker. The school was practically dripping in decorations, and they really weren't helping his mood. He almost felt sorry for how blind everyone was right now. Love didn't last—he was learning that firsthand. His parents had been married for more than twenty years, and even they were splitting up. These high-school relationships weren't going to last forever, and it was kind of sad how everyone thought they would.

The only good thing that had happened to him so far this morning was Andy agreeing to hang out and play pool later. Hiding out in the basement and forgetting all about his parents, the divorce, and this forced holiday that only made people do phony things was all he cared about. At least Jade agreed that they weren't going to be all lovey-dovey or anything—especially now that his parents' split was so new.

Thank God for Andy's basement. He just wanted to be out of the house when his mom got picked up for her date with Mr. Niles. That was one thing he really didn't want to witness. Talk about painful. There should be a holiday for people who had broken hearts, like his dad, not the ones in love, who didn't need more cause for celebration.

Evan turned the corner and caught sight of Jade at her locker. He smiled as he took in the way her knee-length red skirt and pink T-shirt showed off her perfectly toned legs and arms. She really did look great. He loved that she had an athlete's figure— muscular and not too skinny like so many of the girls at SVH. He kept staring for a moment, then it occurred to him that something seemed off. His eyes went from Jade to the hallway around her, and then it sank in. Red skirt, pink T-shirt. Jade was wearing Valentine's colors. What was that about?

He frowned, unsure what to think. Wasn't Jade with him on boycotting this stupid holiday? He'd been sure she was.

Maybe it's an accident, he thought. Jade was a pretty funky dresser, so it was possible that she'd just thrown on the skirt and top without even thinking about the holiday.

Just as he was about to walk over, the girl standing at the locker next to Jade's let out a little squeal. Evan noticed a student-council member decked out in major Valentine's gear talking to her and saw that he'd just delivered a candygram to her. The girl flipped back her brown hair and read the card attached, then giggled and passed it on to her friend.

Evan shook his head. What a relief to be dating someone who wasn't such a girly-girl. He looked at Jade, but his eyes widened when he saw she was staring at the girl and her friend with an expression that seemed almost *wistful*. Her eyes were glued to the candygram. Then suddenly she turned away and switched her gaze back to her locker, her shoulders sagging.

Evan winced. Was she actually hoping for one of those silly bags of candy? Had she thought the guy from the student government had come to deliver one to *her*?

Jade was intently focused on loading her backpack up with books. She hadn't seen him standing there. Evan had meant to go over to her and say good morning, even happy Valentine's Day if he could muster it, but now he couldn't seem to move.

He hadn't been prepared for that look of disappointment on Jade's face. Maybe she did want a big, meaningful celebration today. Maybe all girls did.

She must have just been telling him that she wasn't into Valentine's Day for his sake—because she knew that he was hurting. She deserved a great holiday with cards, poems, and flowers.

He felt a stab of guilt and turned to hurry in the other direction before Jade caught sight of him. The hallway was filled with students trying to get to class, their lockers, or their significant others.

He just couldn't deal with this right now. He'd catch up with her later. Like after Valentine's Day.

Happy Valentine's Day, Maria Slater thought as she made her way toward homeroom. There was no reason for her not to be happy today. It was the most romantic day of the year, and she had an amazing boyfriend. But she and Ken had decided to let this holiday pass in a low-key way since they were both short on cash. They'd agreed that it would be best for both of them not to buy each other gifts for more than ten dollars. Besides, they were solid enough not to have to play into this day of making up for things they'd forgotten all year. It's not like she needed some cheesy stuffed animal to be convinced of Ken's love. They'd gotten way beyond all of that.

So why couldn't she stop frowning, then? Maria sighed, quickening her pace. It would just be nice to

25

have some special present or surprise waiting for her. She'd seen all the gifts being given and received in the halls, and she couldn't help feeling just a teeny bit sad about her and Ken's pact. Maybe she'd been wrong to tell Ken that she didn't want *any* presents.

At least she had tonight to look forward to. She and Ken planned to have a picnic at the beach, and they were spending ten dollars each on food for that. Just the two of them under the stars. That was all they needed, right?

"Hey, Maria!" She glanced up and saw her friend Kristen Kirchner from drama club walking by with her boyfriend, Gene. They were holding hands, and Kristen had a big heart of chocolates tucked under her arm. "Happy Valentine's Day!" Kristen announced with a bright smile.

"Yeah, you too," Maria said, a little wistfully. Kristen and Gene hadn't been together that long, but it looked like the V-day spirit had even gotten to them. Gene gave Kristen a kiss on the cheek and then walked ahead, leaving Kristen to walk with Maria.

"Isn't Valentine's Day the best?" Kristen asked, her cheeks glowing. Maria forced a nod. "I knew you'd understand," Kristen gushed. "Only a couple of my friends have boyfriends right now, so the others aren't really in the mood for this. So, has Ken surprised you with anything yet today?"

"No, we decided not to give each other gifts," Maria said, pulling her books close to her chest. "We're broke."

Kristen's mouth opened a little bit. She looked like she'd just heard that Ken and Maria broke up. "Oh, well, I'm sure you'll still have fun. It's not all about the presents, right?" she said.

"Right," Maria replied, without much enthusiasm.

"Well, see you in drama," Kristen said. "I'll save you some chocolates."

"Yeah, see you," Maria called as she walked in the door of room 212.

There were still a few minutes until the bell, and the room was only half filled. Maria walked toward her desk, then stopped a couple of feet away, letting out a small gasp.

Are those really for me? she wondered in awe.

There on her desk was a huge bouquet of flowers in a glass vase. There were red and pink roses, lilies, and greens spilling over the sides. The arrangement was beautiful and must have cost a small fortune! Ken had left things for her on her desk before, like her favorite candy bar and little notes, but nothing like this.

Maria couldn't help smiling, even though she

knew she wasn't supposed to need this proof of Ken's affection. Ken obviously hadn't followed through on their deal. He knew her so well that he'd seen right through her claim about not wanting a present. And he'd gotten her one anyway!

She walked toward the desk and pulled the card from one of the stems. The note simply read: *To my valentine*. It was perfect, and Ken was perfect for doing something so sweet. Maria buried her nose in the arrangement and inhaled the sweet scent of the flowers.

"They're gorgeous," commented Lisa Weiss, the girl who sat next to Maria in homeroom. Maria looked up at her, still smiling, and then noticed that Lisa seemed a little sad. Sort of the way Maria had felt minutes earlier. But she knew that Lisa's boyfriend, Chris Wolsch, would definitely do something special for Lisa.

"I wish Chris would do something romantic like that for me today," Lisa said, as if she'd heard Maria's thoughts. "I think he managed to forget what day it is. And I don't feel like having to remind him. He either remembers or he doesn't. He's on his own."

Maria smiled. "Yeah, well, I wasn't even supposed to get a gift today. We agreed."

"Guess all bets are off," Lisa said. "With a bouquet like that, you better get him something good in return."

Maria's smile faded. She was such an idiot—she hadn't even thought of that. But she couldn't *not* reciprocate with a gift for Ken. He might not have meant it when he said he was broke, but she did. She had next to no money for a gift, especially not for one as expensive as the flowers must have been.

She was glad Lisa had said something. She might have just taken the flowers and included an extra something special for the picnic, but that wasn't good enough. This called for shelling out some cash. But for what? She'd have to do some serious digging into her savings to afford the present, but first she had to figure out what to even get.

"Oh, no," she muttered, sinking down into her seat.

The smell of the flowers nearly overwhelmed her as she sat, but now it was almost making her feel sick. They were beautiful, but they meant she was in trouble. After all, she only had a few hours to think of the perfect gift for Ken. She looked up at the clock. The school day started in a couple of minutes. There was no time for a trip to the mall—not that she'd even know what to get him. There were a lot more things for guys to give girls on Valentine's Day than the other way around.

What could she do? She looked around the room for inspiration. Every girl was eyeing her bouquet—

even the teacher. "Maria, those are beautiful," Mrs. Fiedler said, smiling. "Someone must like you a lot."

"Thanks," Maria said weakly. "Yeah, they're from my boyfriend."

"Well, then I don't even need to wish you a happy Valentine's Day. You're already having one." She sat down and picked up the attendance sheet.

We'll see about that, Maria thought. Valentine's Day had already gone from depressing to exciting to stressful—and it had barely gotten started.

Will Simmons

Melissa,

I know we've been through a lot this year, which is why this Valentine's Day is so special. I can't wait for all the Valentine's Days we'll have together in the future. I hope you like what I have planned for tonight. Wear something nice and I'll pick you up at seven.

Love,

Will

CHAPTER 3
The Valentine Scorecard

If I see one more bouquet of flowers, I'm going to scream, Jade thought as she sat in history, waiting for class to start. *I can't believe Evan didn't even stop over to say hi before school started.* Seeing Val Morano get that candygram had hurt more than she'd expected. She really needed Evan to do something special for her today—no matter how small.

She knew that he had been distracted lately and things had been really rough for him. But there was no way he could have forgotten it was Valentine's Day.

She finally had a great boyfriend on this stupid holiday, but they had nothing planned for tonight, and it didn't look like any flowers or cards were coming her way either. Didn't Evan know that this was an important day for couples? Jade slumped down in her chair. This was bigger than birthdays and Christmas. Bigger even than anniversaries. In terms of being a couple, Valentine's Day was pretty much the biggest day of all. For guys *and* girls.

Wait, that was it. Jade sat up a little straighter in her seat. It was an important day for couples, *both* parts of the couple. There was no reason why she had to expect a gift and not give Evan anything in return. After all, Valentine's Day wasn't a one-sided deal. So maybe if she got into the spirit, it would help Evan come around.

One problem, Jade realized with a frown. She had no idea what to actually do. She wasn't used to this couple stuff. She'd never had a serious boyfriend before, at least not for this long. And Evan was no ordinary boyfriend either. Plus his parents were in the middle of splitting up, so she knew she had to be very careful.

"Hey, Jade." Jessica Wakefield breezed by Jade and sank into the seat across from her, flashing her a quick smile. As always, Jessica looked great even this early in the morning. Her shoulder-length blond hair was brushed to shining perfection, and her blue-green eyes practically sparkled. Well, Jessica had a reason to be happy. No doubt her boyfriend, Jeremy, had already done some amazingly sweet thing for her. The two of them were borderline sickening.

But Jessica could still be cool, and she was also usually full of advice. *And she knows Evan pretty well.*

33

"Hey, Jessica," Jade said, pulling Jessica's attention away from her notebook. "I need your help."

Jessica tilted her head. "Sure, what's up? Oh, yeah, happy Valentine's Day," she added with another wide smile.

"You too," Jade said, trying not to cringe. "Actually, that's what I need your help on." She tucked a strand of black hair behind her ear. "I'm not really sure if I should do something for Evan. With his parents splitting up, he's not really into the whole love-will-last-forever thing."

Jessica nodded. "Yeah, I guess it's bad timing for him to have a big romantic holiday. That's too bad about his parents—the Plummers always seemed so happy. I guess you never know what's really going on with couples. But you guys are doing okay now, right?"

"Oh, sure, totally," Jade said. "We're fine. I'm just not sure what that means for today, you know? He's freaked about his parents' news, and I don't want to do anything to upset him, but we are a couple even if his parents aren't anymore." Jade glanced around the room, realizing she should lower her voice. The last thing she needed was news of Evan's parents spreading around the school. Evan was a pretty private person.

"You know what I think?" Jessica said. "You

should do what feels right and trust your instincts since neither of us can read Evan's mind."

"I wish I could," Jade said, doodling hearts in the margin of her notebook paper.

"Maybe keep it low-key," Jessica advised. "That's what Jeremy and I are planning. So many couples plan a big expensive dinner or something over the top, but we're just gonna be our usual silly selves."

"What are you doing?" Jade asked, looking for any good ideas that Jessica could throw her way.

"Well, after that horrible surprise party, I knew Fantasy Island Fun House was out—probably forever. But we decided to go to a different arcade in Big Mesa. No fancy clothes tonight, just jeans and T-shirts." Jessica smiled. "It's fine with me."

Jade couldn't help feeling a twinge of envy. Jeremy was so good at this stuff. It wasn't that Jade wished she was still with him—she was so much happier with Evan than she'd ever been during the time she and Jeremy briefly dated. But Jeremy probably had all kinds of things planned out for Jessica, and Evan . . . well, Evan was just different.

"I feel like we've got a fresh start now," Jessica continued. "It's going really well."

Jade managed a small smile and a "great" before sinking back deeper into her state of depression. Everything always worked out for Jessica and for her twin, Elizabeth. But in Jade's world, it didn't work that way. Perfect relationships didn't just float into her life and land on her lap.

So far today she hadn't even gotten a hello from Evan. She couldn't help but wonder if they'd ever be as solid as Jessica and Jeremy or all the other couples at Sweet Valley High. All the other couples who were celebrating Valentine's Day like they were supposed to.

Nine-fifty. It was 9:50 A.M., and Maria still had no idea what to get Ken. All she could do was stare at the clock. Nothing Mr. Ford was saying right now was registering. It was like the teacher and everyone else in the class was on mute, even the guys sitting behind her who'd been whispering about something for the past ten minutes. The worst part was that since everyone in her homeroom had seen the flowers, she'd been getting comments from all the girls (and even some guys) on how pretty they were. They'd only made her feel more guilty that she had nothing for Ken.

He obviously went out of his way to make sure she had the flowers first thing this morning, and she wanted him to have a V-day treat right away as well. So far, she had a list of all his favorite things but still no clue about what to actually get him. There was a gift certificate to his favorite CD store, but she'd have to leave school for that. Football was on the list, of course, but she couldn't get tickets now because it wasn't football season.

What she needed to figure out was what was the guy equivalent to flowers? Cologne? A plant? Nope. This was turning out to be even harder than she had thought it would be.

The bell was about to ring to signal the end of the period. The whispering behind Maria was getting louder, and she started to tune in to what the guys, John Maksel and Brian Cogley, were saying.

"So what am I going to do with the tickets, then? It's such a waste," John said. "And my dad knows the band's manager, so they're really good seats, on the floor."

"I wish I could help you, man," Brian replied. "But my family would kill me if I bailed on visiting my grandmother this weekend. Have you asked the other guys?"

"I've asked everyone I know." John sighed.

Maria held back a smile. She barely knew John and Brian, but they'd been on the football team with Ken. Brian was a big burly center, and the image of him traveling off to visit his grandmother instead of going to a concert with his friends was pretty funny.

"You know, I think my neighbor likes The Friction," Brian offered.

Maria shot up in her seat. The Friction! They were one of Ken's favorite groups. Maria couldn't believe her luck. What were the chances of her sitting in front of a guy who had floor seats to one of the hottest shows in town? She had to say something—fast, before someone else snatched up those tickets.

She breathed in sharply. But what did they cost? Probably a ton, and definitely more than she had on her right now, which was about seven dollars. She could probably pay John back later, though. And she could splurge just this once, right? After all, it was Valentine's Day and it was Ken. She smiled to herself and nodded slowly, then turned to Brian and John as soon as Mr. Ford's back was to them.

"Hey, guys, I kind of heard part of your conversation," she confessed. "But I think I can help you."

"Really? Do you want to buy the tickets?" John asked, leaning forward in his seat.

"Uh, yeah. I do, actually. Are they for this weekend?" Maria asked, pulling her planner out of her backpack.

"Yeah," he replied. "Saturday night at eight at the stadium. They're great seats but kind of expensive."

"How much?" Maria asked, bracing herself for

the damage. She had to pay whatever he asked. This was too perfect, and she was officially out of options.

"Well, they were seventy-five dollars each, but I'll let you have them for a hundred dollars for the pair," he said.

A hundred dollars! Maria almost choked but found herself writing down the date and time in her planner.

"Okay," she said, trying to sound casual. "Uh, thanks," she said, looking up at John.

"Great!" he said. He looked relieved that Maria agreed to the price. She wondered if she could have bargained him down, but it was too late now. Besides, it was almost time to get to her next class.

"I don't have the cash on me today, but I'd like to give the tickets to Ken as a Valentine's Day gift," Maria said. "Can I give you the money tomorrow?"

"Sure, I know where you sit," John said with a grin. "That's a really cool gift to give Ken, you know. He's a lucky guy."

Maria felt a small blush creep over her cheeks. Yeah, Ken was lucky—lucky that his girlfriend hadn't thought things through in time so she was forced to shell out big money for his gift!

"Hey, Ken's in my calc class," Brian piped up as the bell rang and everyone stood up and started to gather their books to leave. "I promise not to say anything, though, since it's a surprise."

This was working out better than Maria could have planned—minus the hefty price tag. She now had someone to help deliver the tickets just the way Ken had left the flowers for her. Ken was going to be so excited about the chance to see The Friction live.

"Actually, can you do me a favor, Brian?" Maria asked.

"Sure. What's that?" he asked, shoving his notebook in his bag.

"Can you give the tickets to Ken special delivery?" Maria tore a sheet of paper out of her notebook and began scribbling a note to Ken.

"Yeah," Brian replied. "But don't you want to give them to him yourself?"

"No. Let's just say I'm already behind in the gift-giving department," she said, handing him the folded paper with the tickets inside.

"Oh, I see, the Valentine's Day scorecard. Glad I'm single." Brian shook his head.

Maria had to laugh. A few minutes ago she was almost wishing the same thing. But now she was so relieved and sure that Ken would love her gift. Plus they had to be even now.

* * *

Don't back down now, he thought as he watched the girl open her locker door and take some books out from inside. Everything about her was so amazing. The way she casually brushed her hair out of her face, the way she smiled at everyone who walked by her, even people she didn't know that well. He missed that smile. He hadn't realized how much until recently.

Valentine's Day was definitely the perfect time to let her know that he wanted her back. It was a little corny, but it gave him a good excuse to just pop in out of the blue. Maybe taking her by surprise would help ease some of the awkwardness too. After all—it had been so long since they were together.

But she'd had so much going on since then, and so had he. It wasn't like he'd sat around pining for her. He'd dated a few girls—even had one pretty serious girlfriend last summer. But somehow none of them had measured up. The big question on his mind was, Would it be as perfect as it had been before? He was pretty sure that the answer was yes. And he was certainly ready to find out. He shot one last glance at her over at her locker, then turned to head off to class. He was going to have to get back to work on that card for her.

Melissa, not Erika, Melissa, not Erika, Will said to himself as he grabbed some books out of his locker

41

between classes. He shouldn't have to chant this stupid mantra over and over. He had the perfect night planned and the perfect girlfriend to share it with. Why was he obsessing over some hot older girl who would never even go out with him anyway?

Will sighed and shoved his calc book into his bag. He looked back toward his locker to see if he'd gotten everything he needed until lunch. He caught sight of the box of candy he'd dropped off when he got to school earlier. First chance he had, he needed to track Melissa down and wish her a happy Valentine's Day. She hardly ever ate stuff like chocolate, but when she did, Will liked to get her the good kind from the fancy store in the mall. He reached up and took the box from his shelf. Might as well carry it with him so that he could give it to her when they ran into each other.

It was a little weird that she hadn't caught up with him before now. He'd walked the route he knew she took between French and European history, but there was no sign of her. Will could only hope she wasn't sick at home in bed or something. That would really ruin his plans for the night.

He threw his bag over one shoulder, turned, and practically plowed down Melissa, who he hadn't realized was standing right next to him.

"Hey!" he said, surprised to see her standing

there so silently. How long had she just been waiting there for him to notice her? She usually wasn't so quiet, and she always had her crew with her—Cherie, Gina, and the other cheerleaders. Something was definitely up.

Will decided to ignore it and gave her a kiss on the cheek. "Happy Valentine's Day," he whispered in her ear as he pulled away. She smelled great.

"Happy Valentine's Day," Melissa said, smiling.

Will's heart swelled. She really was a different person lately. And he couldn't wait for tonight. Suddenly, looking at Melissa right now, he realized what an idiot he was to think about Erika at all. Yeah, Erika was new and exciting, but he loved Melissa. They just *fit* together. They had a history—and a future.

"So, are you excited to see what I have planned for tonight?" Will grinned.

Melissa's face scrunched up into a guilty expression, and Will felt his chest tighten. Now what?

"Oh, right," Melissa said, eyeing him cautiously with her lips still pressed together. "Actually, that's what I needed to talk to you about. I can't make it tonight." She paused, staring up at him with those bright blue eyes. "But we can celebrate over the weekend, right?"

What?! Today was Valentine's Day, not this

43

weekend. He'd made all those plans . . . and she knew that. How could she do this to him? He'd been talking about this night for weeks. Will took a deep breath. The last thing he wanted to do was lose it in the hallway. Besides, Melissa had to have a great explanation as to why she was canceling. Like emergency surgery or a death in the family. Will was on the verge of exploding, but he decided to keep his mouth shut and let Melissa finish her explanation of why she was blowing him off.

"I have this family thing that just came up," she said, looking around the hallway. "My uncle Phil lives in France, but he's in town on business tonight, and my parents are making me go to dinner with the family. They said something about it a couple of weeks ago, but I forgot until today."

Will looked at Melissa in horror. That was it? His girlfriend was dumping him on Valentine's Day for a family dinner that she'd known about for weeks? And worse, Melissa was done explaining, and she didn't seem sorry in the least. Just flashing her fake-guilty face, waiting to be forgiven and pulled into a big hug, like always. His face burned, and his fists clenched at his sides. He opened his mouth to speak, knowing it would be hard to keep his voice down.

"Hey, Melissa! Come on. We've gotta get to

physics!" Cherie Reese was running down the hall. She grabbed Melissa's hand and smiled in Will's face. "Sorry to break up your little love fest. Let's go!" she said, pulling on Melissa's hand.

"Right! I'll talk to you later," Melissa said over her shoulder as Cherie practically dragged her down the hall.

Will stood there a minute, stunned. Then he turned and slammed his open locker door shut. Hard. The metal clanged and shook for a few seconds.

He couldn't believe that Melissa wasn't putting him first—again. And this day of all days was the one where it really mattered. Here he had the whole thing planned, thanks to Erika, and Melissa couldn't even tell him that she had a family dinner coming up? She couldn't have checked to make sure there wouldn't be a conflict? But the real kicker was that she didn't even seem sorry. If Will had canceled their date, he never would have heard the end of it and would be making up for it for weeks. Unbelievable.

Will opened up his bag as the bell rang. Now, to top it all off, he was late for class. He grabbed the box of chocolates and clutched the gold box tightly in his hand. He passed a trash can on his way to class and tossed the box inside. He had wasted more time and money in the past few days than he wanted to think about.

And what for? Nothing. Absolutely nothing. Will shook his head as he walked through the door to class. He was late, but he didn't care.

Valentine's Day was starting to leave a sour taste in his mouth.

Jeremy Aames

Dear Jess,

This is the happiest Valentine's Day I've ever had. Actually, every day I'm with you is the best—yeah, I know, the cheese-o-meter is going off. Sorry, but it's true. We've been through a lot, and we've both done some stupid stuff, but we're still together—because we're right for each other. I hope that never changes. Happy Valentine's Day.

Love,
Jeremy

CHAPTER
The Secret Plan

4

"Amazing. That's so romantic," Jessica said to Tia as they walked down the hall together. "He actually showed up here and left you a note on your locker?"

Tia restrained a groan. Like Andy, Jessica had just assumed the guy behind the note had to be Trent. How could they not get that Tia needed to move on? It was over with Trent. Not in any of her friends' minds, though.

"Admit it, Tee. You're a little bit impressed by it—and him," Jessica pushed.

Tia shrugged. She had heard the hope in Jessica's voice. More than anyone, Jessica wanted Tia to forgive Trent and give him another chance. Probably because Jessica still felt guilty for what had happened, even though it really wasn't her fault. But maybe she figured if Tia and Trent got back together, she could finally stop feeling bad.

Still, no matter what was behind her friends' reasons for thinking she and Trent should be a couple,

Tia wasn't buying it. After all, if he'd been tempted to stray once, he'd probably get interested in another girl if they got back together. Plus everyone kept forgetting that she had absolutely no proof that Trent was definitely her secret admirer. Although even she had to admit that he did seem like the most obvious person.

"I'm still not totally sure it was Trent," Tia reminded Jessica anyway. They passed the front office, and Tia put her bag down on the bench outside the principal's door for a second, resting her foot up on the bench so she could tie her shoelace. When she'd finished, she glanced through the double doors leading into the front office. The school must've been all heart for Valentine's Day because there was actually no poor freshman sitting scared on the chairs outside the principal's office, in trouble for throwing spit wads in class or something. That was a change. Jessica gave Tia a light tug on the arm. "Who else would it be?" she said. "It has to be Trent."

"Yeah, I guess there aren't too many possibilities right now," Tia admitted with a shrug. Kind of pathetic that there was only one logical choice. Only one guy who might want to be with her for Valentine's Day.

She grabbed her bag and started to walk down the hall again. Jessica walked alongside her, obviously not done with her case yet.

"It's not anyone else," Jessica said. "Why not just admit that you want it to be Trent, just like he wants to be with you?"

"Tia! Hey, Tia, wait a second," a voice called from down the hall.

Tia turned to see a sophomore from the debate team waving her arms over her head. Tia knew it was Valentine's Day and everyone was in a good mood, but this greeting was a bit much from someone she hardly knew.

The girl ran toward Tia and Jessica. "Hey, there's a delivery for you in the front office," she said, slightly breathless. "I saw you walk by and thought I'd let you know."

Tia frowned, confused. What could have been delivered to the front office for her?

Something else from Trent, maybe? The thought popped into her head, and her heart skipped a beat. *So what if it is?* she thought quickly. She didn't want anything else from him. She didn't want anything to do with him, right?

"Okay, thanks," she managed to get out, trying to turn down the internal volume. "I guess I'll check it out."

"See ya!" the girl chirped before taking off down the hall.

Tia turned toward Jessica, her eyebrows raised.

"Don't give me that look," Jessica said. She turned and headed back to the office. "Come on, let's go see what you got." Watching Jessica walk, Tia could finally understand that expression about someone having a "bounce" to their step.

Tia trailed behind her friend, trying to ignore the building anticipation. It didn't matter even if it *was* something from Trent. None of this changed anything.

So then why am I hoping it's from him?

She wasn't. She wasn't hoping anything.

Jessica opened the heavy wood door and held it for Tia. The linoleum squeaked under Tia's sneakers, and she couldn't help but get that sinking feeling in her stomach as she walked in. She hadn't been sent to the principal's office in years, but she felt like she was in trouble for some reason anyway. She just wanted to get her delivery and go.

Tia walked up to the counter and cleared her throat. The receptionist's back was to them as she typed on her computer. She turned around as soon as she realized someone was behind her. "Hello, can I help you?" she asked.

"I was told there was a delivery for me. I'm Tia Ramirez."

"Ooh, yes." The woman breathed in sharply and smiled. "We were just about to make an announcement

51

that you should come and pick them up," she said, pointing to the end of the counter.

There amid a sea of manila folders was a glass vase tied with a pink ribbon. Inside were six red roses and ivy. A card was taped to the vase.

"Wow!" Jessica whispered. "*Someone* is trying pretty hard."

Tia walked toward the flowers and bit her lip. They were beautiful. Were they really from Trent?

Her heart pounded a little harder as she opened the card and read it: *Are you convinced that we belong together yet? Love, Your Hopeful Valentine.*

Tia couldn't believe it. A card was one thing, but flowers like this on Valentine's Day were really expensive.

"What does it say?" Jessica demanded, already reading over Tia's shoulder. She let out a small sigh. "I wish I would get a delivery like that from Jeremy," she said. "You're going to forgive Trent now, right?"

Tia didn't respond. It was too much to take in at once. Why was he doing this?

"Look at all he's done today. The card, the flowers," Jessica continued. She seemed so anxious for Tia to just give in.

But it's too little, too late, Tia thought. She had her pride.

"Here," she said, handing Jessica the vase. "Now

you don't need Jeremy to get you flowers—you can have these."

"Tia, I'm not taking your flowers," Jessica said, trying to hand them back. "You're just being stubborn. Enjoy them."

Tia shook her head. "The card and the flowers can't change the way I feel. There's absolutely no way I'm taking Trent back—even if he delivered a new car to the Sweet Valley parking lot."

Jessica frowned. "Why can't you just give him another chance?"

The bell rang, and Tia felt another cliché come to mind. *Saved*, she thought. She had a free period now, but she knew Jessica was on her way to class.

"We'll talk at lunch," Jessica said before turning to rush down the hall.

Tia nodded but hoped the whole thing would be forgotten by then. Jessica had managed to push the vase back into her hands before taking off. She stared at the flowers a second, then leaned her head toward them. Wow. They smelled so fresh and clean. She had to remind herself not to enjoy them, though. She couldn't accept an expensive gift like this from someone she wasn't even dating and wouldn't date again. She and Trent were through.

Why did he have to try so hard? She allowed herself one more whiff of the bouquet before putting it back on the counter and leaving the office. She was sure that the receptionist would enjoy it. She sighed and turned toward her locker. Trent's gestures really were sweet, even if she couldn't take him back.

Ken's stomach grumbled as he headed into calculus, his last class before lunch. He was really looking forward to that picnic he and Maria were going to have later on. She always prepared a feast for their beach picnics.

He was in charge of dessert and drinks. As a special treat, he'd gotten a bottle of sparkling cider and chocolate-covered strawberries. He hoped Maria would be impressed. They were planning to take a blanket and head to their favorite spot. If it turned out to be a clear night, then they'd be able to see the moon reflect on the water. Total romance. The perfect place to be alone.

"Yo, Ken." Ken looked up and saw Brian Cogley hovering over his desk.

"Hey," Ken replied, wondering what was up. They hadn't talked much since the football season ended.

"Got something for you," Brian said, handing Ken a folded-up piece of paper.

"What's this?" Ken asked, taking the paper from Brian's outstretched hand.

"Uh, it's not from me, man," Brian joked. "Maria

was in my class earlier this morning, and she wanted me to do the cupid thing and deliver this to you."

Ken grinned sheepishly. He loved Maria's notes, and it was a nice idea to have someone deliver her valentine to Ken. He'd been missing her all day and hadn't even gotten the chance to wish her a happy Valentine's Day yet. He had a card for her later tonight that was still in his locker.

"Thanks," Ken said.

Brian winked. "Let me know if there's a reply you need me to make," he said with a smile. "Hey, I should have thought to charge for my services." He took his seat at the front of the classroom.

Ken chuckled. He opened the note, and two small pieces of paper fell to the floor. His brow furrowed, he leaned down to pick them up. They actually looked like tickets. Movie tickets, maybe? He grabbed them and took a closer look.

Oh, there's no way, he thought, almost choking. In his hands were two tickets to The Friction, one of his favorite bands. Floor seats too. They must have cost *serious* money.

Ken looked at Maria's note, reading it quickly, anxious for an explanation. Maybe she had won them or someone had been more than generous and given them to her. But who would give up these seats? Maria's note was sweet but vague. She said she knew that he wouldn't let the day go by without a gift of some sort. So here was hers to him. Happy Valentine's Day.

Yeah, happy Valentine's. Ken's stomach sank. He couldn't believe that Maria had sprung for these tickets after they had agreed not to exchange presents. He was psyched to see The Friction and all, but what was she doing?

What she was doing was expecting a nice gift in return, like she had hinted in her note, Ken thought. He ran a hand through his short blond hair and leaned back in his chair.

A few minutes ago Valentine's Day had been a happy day, with only a simple, romantic, and inexpensive picnic planned. Now he had no idea what he was supposed to do. And what did her note mean, exactly? Ken wasn't sure, but their pact was obviously meaningless.

He checked his watch and cringed. It was all too much to handle right now before a calc quiz he'd spent half the night cramming for.

He did have lunch next period. He'd been planning to hang out with Maria and eat a big meal. His stomach growled again, but he'd have to go hungry today. Or pick up something fast at the mall.

He could buy her those earrings she had seen and wanted last time they'd been there. They were pricey, but what could he do? He didn't want to disappoint Maria. Not on Valentine's Day.

Ken looked down at the tickets in his hand again. They were for Saturday night, and they had cost seventy-five dollars each. He whistled under his breath. They definitely hadn't been cheap.

Maria really had been bluffing when she said "no gifts." This was one of the nicest presents he'd ever received. He had to do the same for her and buy her a gift she'd remember forever.

He needed to pull out all the stops.

Melissa smiled to herself. This was going to be one of the best tricks she'd ever pulled off. She really was an amazing actress, telling Will that she was busy tonight. She'd just thought up her excuse at the last minute, but he had definitely been convinced by her performance. She could tell by the look on his face.

Before Cherie had pulled her away, she had been tempted to tell Will that she was kidding and she couldn't wait for tonight. She just couldn't take that disappointed glint in his eyes. But now she was glad that she hadn't.

She had plans of her own for tonight, and they included a big surprise for Will. It had been hard to sit through class, imagining how the night was going to turn out. The trademark grin he'd flash when she showed up out of the blue and the great time they'd have laughing about her trick later.

Finally the bell rang and pulled her from her thoughts. Melissa grabbed her books and hurried out the door.

That had been her last class before lunch. She couldn't wait to brag to her friends about everything she was doing for Will. True, they knew she had something up her sleeve because she'd teased them earlier that week by hinting about a great idea. But she was waiting until she put her plan into motion before she filled them all in. She speeded up the walk toward her locker.

Just as she rounded the corner, she caught sight of them down the hall. Cherie, Amy Sutton, Lila Fowler, and Gina Cho were all hanging out at Melissa's locker, just like they always did before lunch. She smiled as she approached them.

"Hey, Melissa," Amy greeted her first.

"Hey, guys," Melissa said. She reached over casually to open her locker and stuff the books inside.

"So, are you finally going to tell us about your big plan for tonight?" Amy pushed.

Melissa just kept smiling. "I don't know—what are you guys all doing?" she asked. *Save the best for last,* she thought.

58

"Well, Eric and I are going to dinner at The Beachfront Hotel with his sister and her boyfriend," Amy replied, her eyes shining with excitement. "It's that really nice white hotel with pillars on the beach," she added, as if Melissa wouldn't know.

"That sounds great," Melissa said, still not volunteering any info. She was just going to listen patiently to everyone else's story before she told her own.

"I've got a date with a freshman at SVU," Lila piped up.

Gina laughed, catching Melissa's eye. "She's going out with Warren Martell. Remember him?"

Melissa's smile began to border on a smirk. "Of course," she said.

"He's the guy who almost got expelled from El Carro last year for his senior prank," Cherie explained to Lila.

Lila's cheeks flushed, but she tossed her dark hair back behind her shoulder with a typical Lila gesture of "I'm above you all anyway." Lila was a real classic. Melissa found her very amusing, most of the time, at least.

"That was last *year*," Lila pointed out. "At least I've moved on from high-school boys."

Melissa tried not to roll her eyes. Her friends always thought it was a competition to see who could date the best-looking or oldest guy or whatever, but their relationships never worked out. They'd never had anything like she had with Will.

"Okay, it's your turn," Cherie said, turning back to Melissa. "What are you and Will doing anyway?"

Melissa shut her locker, waiting patiently until she had everyone focused on her. "Well, Will had something special planned, but I told him I'm busy tonight, so he has to cancel," she said.

Four confused pairs of eyes stared back at her.

"What? You're not going to be with Will on Valentine's Day?" Amy demanded.

Melissa loved moments like this, when her friends were hanging on her every word. She breathed in. "No," she said slowly. Cherie's mouth dropped open slightly.

"Not doing what he wants to do." Melissa raised her eyebrows a fraction. "Of course, we'll be together. I just told him that I couldn't make it tonight so I could surprise him at his internship instead and take him to a very special dinner."

"Ooh! That's perfect," Amy squealed.

"Pretty romantic." Cherie nodded in agreement.

Lila gave her hair another flip. "I think you're crazy for not letting him pay and take you to dinner himself," she said.

Melissa shrugged. "I want Will to know that I can

make an effort too. And once he finds out what I've done for him, he'll be *very* grateful." She shook her head. "You just have to think these things through a little better," she chided, enjoying the way Lila's expression darkened.

"Whatever," Lila said. "We'd better get to lunch."

Melissa followed the others as they headed toward the cafeteria. Too bad she'd forgotten that her friends weren't quite at her level and they just wouldn't get how exciting her idea was. After tonight Will would be back eating out of her hand. Lately he'd been a little too distracted by this whole internship thing, and that was a problem.

But now she'd have a chance to see the *Tribune* office and remind Will how much more important their relationship was than some silly newspaper job. She'd stand out against the boring, drab walls there. He'd be so surprised at everything she'd done for him that she'd go back to being top priority.

Still, he didn't have to drop the internship completely, and she was looking forward to seeing where he worked. After all, he was building his future. *Their* future. She could already see his byline on major sports stories.

This was just the start of many more Valentine's celebrations between them. She was sure of that.

Jessica Wakefield

Dear Jeremy,

Happy Valentine's Day! Are you ready for a night of fun? I know this night will be perfect, just like all our time together. I'm so happy that you're my valentine!

XO
Jess

CHAPTER
No Turning **5** Back Now

Finally, lunchtime, Andy thought as he walked out of the classroom and headed toward his locker. The one period of the day when he would be able to separate himself from the rest of the student body.

He could hang out, try not to think about what day it was . . . or about Dave. That was pretty much all he had done in his morning classes. It hadn't helped that everyone around him was googly-eyed and in love.

Andy's locker was on the other side of the school, so he had to pass by the glass windows that looked out on the quad. The bright California sunshine was out—of course—and the girls and guys outside looked like they were in some kind of video for a love song. People were holding hands, eating lunch together, and just generally happy. Ewww.

Andy knew that the cafeteria would be no different. There didn't seem to be one single spot on the entire Sweet Valley High campus where he could be alone to wallow in his misery.

It was time to just get out of SVH altogether. Lunch on campus was definitely not happening today. Andy couldn't help but imagine how it would be if he and Dave were one of the happy couples. In public, like everyone else, giving each other valentines and being all goofy. *But that's not happening,* Andy reminded himself. Even if Andy hadn't broken up with Dave, they wouldn't have been able to spend today together, out in the open. Dave couldn't handle anyone—especially his dad—knowing he was gay. Andy could get that, but he couldn't live like that. Not anymore.

Andy opened his locker and threw his books inside, grabbing his lunch bag from the top shelf. He slammed his locker door and took the back way to the parking lot, hoping he didn't have to witness any more V-day happiness on the way.

Fortunately, he didn't run into anyone. Andy got his sunglasses out of his bag and slipped them on. He climbed in his car and sat back in the driver's seat.

Now all he had to do was figure out exactly where he was going. He had no idea. But step one was to drive away from Sweet Valley High.

Andy's spirits lifted a little as he made a left out

of the parking lot. Maybe if he just drove around for a little while, he'd get inspired by a spot and stop to eat. Until then he was content to blast his tunes and try to get the image of Dave out of his head. Andy turned up the volume on his radio and sang along with the new angry rock song, something he would never listen to normally.

Why did he have to fall for a guy who wasn't ready to tell people he was gay? It was almost ironic that it had taken Andy himself a while to come out, to be comfortable with himself and feel like he could date someone. And then of course the first guy he met and liked was an exact version of himself—a few months ago. Scared and embarrassed. But if he had met someone he cared about back then, it might have made Andy more willing to be honest. He had offered to help Dave, but not upsetting his father was obviously more important to him than a relationship with Andy.

Andy's shoulders slumped, and he stared at a group of trees ahead in the distance. Just then a blue Corolla made a left out of a shopping center, cutting Andy off and pulling him back to earth. He'd been completely zoning out. He shook his head and caught sight of the nearest street sign. He'd just driven across town. Aimless driving was not a good thing when he was distracted and bummed out.

Time to stop and eat, he thought. He was near the old park that his family used to go to when Andy was a little kid. He used to play catch with his dad, and they'd have picnics in the summer. They even carved their names on a tree. Pretty cheesy, but those were good times, exactly the kind of things he needed to fill his mind with right now.

Andy turned into the park entrance and cut the engine. If he remembered correctly, there was a group of park benches near the entrance. A good shady spot and a tuna sandwich were about all Andy could handle right now.

As he walked toward a group of benches inside the park entrance, Andy nearly turned back. There was a guy with a hooded sweatshirt sitting on one, and he really didn't feel like having to make small talk right now if the guy wanted to chat. Andy shook his head and took a deep breath. No, it was a free country and a big park. He could manage to enjoy his lunch, right?

He walked slowly toward the bench, approaching the stranger from the side. He could make his way over to the other bench without even having to say hello. Just then the guy looked up and turned toward him. Andy breathed in sharply and felt his knees nearly give out under him.

Dave. Andy squinted and closed his eyes, opening

them quickly to see if he was just imagining things. After all, he'd been thinking about Dave all day. Maybe he was just seeing him because he wished he could. Nope, it was definitely Dave. And Dave had seen Andy as well.

There was no turning back now.

"I can't believe you left those gorgeous flowers in the office for the receptionist," Jessica said, taking a sip of iced tea.

"I know, Tee, isn't that a little extreme?" Elizabeth chimed in.

Tia glanced across the cafeteria table at Elizabeth, surprised that she was backing up her twin on this one. After all, Elizabeth had been burned left and right this year. Tia would have thought she of all people would get why Tia couldn't forgive Trent.

Where were all of her hard-hearted friends to tell her that she was totally right? What was making everyone think that she should get back together with Trent?

"Well, I wasn't going to keep them," Tia insisted. She started picking at the edge of her paper napkin, ripping off tiny pieces. "I mean, after all, that would be like saying this whole thing is working, right? That I'm willing to give Trent another chance." She turned toward Jessica. "It's not happening," she said as firmly as she could.

Jessica frowned slightly and bit her lip. It was getting pretty weird how personally Jessica was taking all of this. But Jessica had to get it through her head that it was over between Tia and Trent. It was time to move on.

"Don't look now, Tia, but I think Trent is trying for strike three," Elizabeth said. She nodded toward an approaching student-council representative wearing the red-and-pink T-shirt that all the candy-gram cupids had on today. She was heading straight toward their table with a look of recognition on her face. It was Jen Lynch, another El Carro transfer.

"Hey, Tia," Jen said, a big smile on her face.

"Hi, Jen. Do you know Elizabeth and Jessica?" Tia asked, pointing toward her friends.

"I think we've met before," Jen said. "I think I saw you with a big bouquet of flowers earlier today."

Jessica blushed slightly, and Tia had to smile. So Jeremy had sent flowers before their date. Jessica must have forgotten to tell her. Tia was glad that her friend seemed so happy. Jessica and Jeremy belonged together.

"But now I have something for you, Tia." Jen pulled a card out of the red box she was carrying. She handed the pink card and a bag of candy kisses to Tia.

"Happy Valentine's Day!" Jen said, giving Tia a little wink.

"You too," Tia said a little less enthusiastically as Jen walked across the cafeteria to deliver some more candygrams.

"Wow! He doesn't give up," Jessica said, her eyes gleaming.

"The guy gets points for persistence, Tee," said Elizabeth, popping a potato chip into her mouth.

"What does it say?" Jessica prompted, leaning forward over the lunchroom table.

Tia swallowed and read the note aloud: "'From someone who had to get a little help to send this to you.'" Her jaw dropped slowly, and she faced her friends.

"Wait a minute. Did you two have something to do with this?" Tia demanded, waving the card in the air.

Elizabeth's and Jessica's eyes got a little bigger, but neither girl opened her mouth. Tia should have known that they were in on it. Only Sweet Valley students were allowed to sign up for the candygrams. But neither of them had said a word. They had both gone behind her back. She couldn't believe it.

"Jessica, spill!" Tia ordered. Her eyes narrowed, and she sat upright in her chair.

Elizabeth jumped in, obviously covering for her

69

sister. "Tia, is it so wrong to want you and Trent to give it another try—in the spirit of the day? His persistence should count for something."

Tia couldn't believe what she was hearing. Were they serious? They'd been in on it all along? Didn't it occur to them that Tia might not *want* Trent to keep trying? That she meant it when she broke up with him?

She could feel the color rising to her cheeks, and she took a deep breath. She had to calm down.

"And by the way, it's not persistence, it's arrogance!" she said, trying not to raise her voice. She stood up and pushed back her chair.

She felt her knees buckle beneath her, and she licked her lips nervously.

She wasn't exactly sure why she was reacting so strongly, especially since part of her couldn't help but think the whole thing was pretty sweet. Mostly it was the idea that no one, not her ex-boyfriend or two of her closest friends, appeared to be taking her seriously. Did they actually expect her to forgive him for cheating on her—with her best friend, no less— just because he sprang for a few chocolate kisses, a Hallmark card, and a bouquet of flowers? She nearly nodded in agreement with herself before she noticed that Jessica and Elizabeth were both watching her carefully, waiting to see what she was about to do.

Basically she didn't have much choice. Sure, part of her was fighting the urge to drive out to Big Mesa and leap into Trent's arms and say, "Of course I forgive you," but she was resolved to stay strong. Especially in front of this audience.

Jessica's face paled, and Elizabeth's eyes were full of concern. She stood up too and moved over to Tia's side.

"Are you okay?" she asked.

"I'm fine," Tia said. She'd made up her mind. She would drive out to Big Mesa. Not to stage a tearful reunion, but to instruct Trent to stop sending her gifts. Plain and simple.

Tia looked down at her oversized watch and thought of Trent. When they first started hanging out, she used to fidget with her old watch out of nervousness. One day it just fell off, and she'd been using her dad's old watch ever since. She made a mental note to replace that little reminder of their relationship as soon as possible and then lifted her bag off the floor. She had exactly twenty-two minutes to make it to Trent's and back before her next class.

"I've gotta go. I'm gonna go to Big Mesa," she said, grabbing her bag from underneath the table. "I need to tell him to stop all of this. He's just wasting his time and money."

Jessica jerked up her head, her eyes wide with panic. "No, Tia—you can't go there," she blurted.

Tia didn't have time to deal with Jessica's horrified expression or listen to another one of Elizabeth's speeches on why she and Trent should get back together. She had to do this now, before she lost her nerve.

Jade popped a french fry in her mouth and looked over at Evan. Normally his eyes followed any junk food on the table. But he seemed distracted, and it was hard not to notice that he hadn't even mentioned what day it was.

She tried to get his attention by sighing loudly, but he didn't notice. His eyes were riveted on a poster of the food pyramid.

"I wonder which food group hummus belongs to."

"Did you say something?" Evan mumbled as he munched away on his falafel sandwich.

Jade felt like she was about to scream. Most boyfriends—the ones who actually wanted to stay with their girlfriends, at least—were making a big deal out of this day. Was it so much to expect a little something from her own boyfriend? Yeah, he'd been going through a lot with his parents' divorce, but that didn't mean he couldn't let himself enjoy his own relationship. And things had been going so well.

For the first time in her life Jade had a reason to be grateful for having lived through her parents' divorce. It made it much easier for her and Evan to talk about his experience—she got everything he was feeling, and he felt reassured knowing that she'd been through it already. But today he wasn't talking at all. It was like she wasn't even there.

The last five minutes without conversation had been painful. Jade needed to break the silence. She cleared her throat.

Finally Evan snapped back to earth.

"Need some water?" he asked. He actually looked concerned.

She shook her head. "Welcome back. You were totally spacing," she said, smiling in spite of herself. It was hard to stay mad at Evan. Even if he was totally dropping the ball on Valentine's Day.

"Sorry," Evan said. He smiled back at Jade, and her heart melted.

"Do you want a fry? They're almost all gone," she said, looking down at her plate. This should have made Evan snap out of his funk. French fries were his absolute favorite. But Evan just shook his head.

Jade's eyebrow shot up. "Are you sure?" she asked. He showed signs of life with a half nod, but his eyes went straight back to the poster.

If Jade had any hope of getting a Valentine's Day

plan going, she had to get some kind of read on Evan's mood. And the only way to do that was to get him talking. "So, how're your classes going?" she asked, licking her lips from all the salt that was on her fries. Lame as it was, it was the best she could come up with under the circumstances. There were another twenty minutes of lunch, and she was going to get an answer on something from Evan. No matter how painful it was.

"Well, Spanish is really tough. Worse than last year's class, and you know how hard that was," Evan offered.

At least Evan was talking, but Jade was still nervous—about him, about their relationship. She picked at her nail polish under the table and tried to focus on what he was saying.

Evan went on and on about his Spanish troubles but made no mention of holiday plans or evenings out. He wasn't avoiding conversation, he was just avoiding conversation about Valentine's Day.

Jade felt crushed. If Evan wanted to see her tonight, he would have mentioned something by now. She blinked back tears.

Did Evan even realize how disappointed she was? If he did, he obviously didn't care.

Suddenly she didn't want to listen to what Evan had to say about his classes. She just wanted to be a million miles away. Or to fast-forward and have this day be over with no remembrance of how disappointed she was.

Jade still had a plate full of food in front of her, minus the fries, but she wasn't hungry anymore. She'd lost her appetite—and any hope of a fun or romantic Valentine's Day.

"What are you doing here?" Andy asked in disbelief, standing before Dave. He tried to keep his voice calm, but it felt like every nerve in his body was on alert. Dave glanced at Andy, and it struck Andy how sad Dave looked, sitting there all alone with the hood on his sweatshirt pulled down over his head and a half-eaten sandwich next to him. He paused before answering Andy, and his silence felt like an eternity. Andy nearly turned around and walked away.

"I come here when I need to think," Dave replied, pulling his hood back so that Andy could see him more clearly. There were dark circles under his eyes, and his mouth formed a thin line, not quite a frown but something close.

Andy wiped his hands on the sides of his jeans and took a deep breath.

"I've done a lot of thinking lately. It's pretty much all I do anymore," Dave said. "I knew this would be hard, but I didn't know it would be this hard. Sometimes I wish I could just go back to dating girls. You know?"

Andy felt his heart squeeze in sympathy. He had felt exactly the same way. He had just wanted to fit in and be like everyone else, and he'd stayed up late at night, wondering if he could force himself to not be gay.

But I couldn't, and neither can Dave, Andy thought. Was Dave sitting here thinking about telling his dad the truth about himself?

Suddenly the bright sunshine on his back wasn't so annoying to Andy. Maybe there was hope for this day.

Dave gave him a half smile. "So, what are you doing here?" he asked.

"The same," Andy said, letting out a chuckle.

Something in the air seemed to change, soften, and Dave motioned for Andy to sit down next to him. Andy hesitated, then started to take a seat but noticed the mess of crumbs on the bench.

He scooped up a crumb and pretended to smell it. "PB&J, huh?" he asked. "I'm a marshmallow-with-PB man myself, but to each his own."

"Crunchy or smooth?" Dave asked.

"Are you kidding? Smooth all the way. What's the point of eating processed food if you can trace it back to its original source?" Andy quipped.

"Good point," Dave agreed with a smile.

Andy brushed away the rest of the mess on the bench and then sat down. He started to unwrap his own sandwich, realizing he was starving. All that food talk must be getting to him.

"So is it valentine overload at your school too?" Dave asked, looking around the park.

"Definitely." Andy swallowed, glancing in the direction that Dave seemed intent on. A group of high-school kids that Andy didn't recognize walked by, laughing. Dave sat back on the bench and then looked behind Andy as the group walked away.

Andy took another bite of his sandwich. He felt Dave's gaze move to him. Their eyes locked, and Andy took a deep breath. He felt a real connection to Dave—he wasn't imagining this.

He knew that Dave was struggling. Maybe he needed to help him through this time rather than turn away. Dave smiled. "This isn't exactly an easy holiday for guys like us, huh?" he asked.

"More like an endurance test than a holiday," Andy admitted.

They laughed, then turned and stared out toward the park. Neither of them said a word. But it was an easy silence, Andy noted. They sat like that for a few seconds, and Andy felt closer to Dave than ever. Maybe they still had a chance.

"I'm glad you're here," Dave said, glancing at Andy out of the corner of his eyes. His mouth was curled up into a smile.

"Me too," Andy said, his heart rate now shooting up. "Pretty lucky, huh?"

"Yeah. It's such a . . ." Dave trailed off.

The same group of kids walked by again, but this time they were closer to Dave and Andy and seemed to be looking over at them.

"A what?" Andy asked. Dave grew quiet and pulled his hood down a little lower. Andy could have sworn he moved away from him on the bench a little bit too.

"Everything okay?" Andy asked.

"Uh, yeah," Dave said. "Why?"

"I don't know. Do you know those kids?" Andy asked, motioning toward them.

"Not really," Dave said. Andy thought he sounded a little nervous, and his leg kept twitching.

Something was definitely up with Dave. Conner had that same leg-twitch thing, and Andy knew that it meant Conner was nervous about something—or someone. Did Dave recognize those kids?

Andy was pretty sure they went to Dave's school. He was also pretty convinced that was why Dave had gotten quiet and distracted. He didn't want to be seen with Andy.

Andy gulped down the bite of tuna he had been chewing on and tossed the rest of his sandwich back in the bag. Dave was already on his feet before Andy could swallow.

"I gotta get back," Dave said, then quickly scanned the park.

Andy felt like yelling at him that he knew what was up, but he felt more sad than angry. Dave couldn't even have lunch in the park without worrying about someone seeing them together.

Andy shook his head and stood up. "No, you stay. I've gotta run anyway."

Dave looked surprised and opened his mouth to speak.

"See ya," Andy said.

"Yeah, bye," Dave said softly, looking down at the ground. But he didn't move.

Happy Valentine's Day, Andy thought as he walked back toward the parking lot. He made sure not to turn back, hoping that would help get the message across—that he was fully aware of how uncomfortable Dave felt when they were in public together and he didn't have to stand for that. He would not be with someone who was embarrassed to be seen with him.

This had to be the worst Valentine's Day in the history of the world. *The only thing worse than not*

*having anyone on Valentine's Day is finding out that
the person you thought could be your valentine isn't.*
Actually, when he gave it some thought, he realized
there was one thing worse than that—*Finding all this
out during lunch period so that you have to get
through an entire afternoon of classes before getting to
go home and retreat into your basement.*

He watched enviously as a couple walked hand in
hand with their picnic basket through the park. This
time last year that could have been him, with some
girl. His heart wouldn't be in it, but his life would at
least be a whole lot less complicated if he had a fe-
male valentine who was psyched at the idea of flowers and a card for Valentine's Day.

Andy turned up the music full blast in his car
and drove away from the park—and away from
Dave.

Dear Valentine,
    Roses are red,
    Violets are blue,
    ~~You don't know much~~ I've been wait-
ing all year
    ~~I like you.~~ To talk to you.

    Meet me at First and Ten tonight at
six. I'll have a red rose.
                        Love,
                        Your Secret Admirer

    It's too much. I'm going to scare
her off. Ugh—this is driving me crazy.

Jade Wu

Dear Evan,

H appy Valentine's Day! I know that this is an especially hard thing for you to celebrate right now, but I wanted you to know that I'm here for you and I know that you'll get through this. We can get through it together, okay? All relationships have their ups and downs, but we can focus on the ups in ours. Starting with, will you be my valentine?

Love,
Jade

What's the point of even giving this to him? Maybe I should just rip it up and throw it away. It's not like I'll be getting one back from <u>him.</u>

CHAPTER
A Low-key Holiday

6

Tia hurried down the hallway, finally piecing together everything that had happened this morning. Suddenly Jessica's excitement over the whole Trent thing made sense. She'd been helping him all along. They'd been planning and scheming about this just like they'd done in setting up Jeremy's birthday party.

Tia knew her face was bright red, and she wanted to calm down before driving over to El Carro, but she didn't have a second to spare.

The whole thing made her want to scream. The girl had some nerve. Here Jessica probably thought she was doing Tia some big favor. If Jessica wanted to do Tia a favor, she would stay as far away from Trent as possible. And if Elizabeth wanted to pitch in, she'd help keep her away.

"Tia! Stop!" Tia turned and saw Jessica running down the hallway, her blond hair flying behind her.

Tia was tempted to keep walking, but she knew

Jessica wouldn't let her get away. This had better be good—and fast. She looked down at her watch again.

Jessica caught up to her, breathless and obviously upset. *Good,* Tia thought. *She's going to apologize. . . .*

Tia crossed her arms over her chest and raised her eyebrows. "What?" she asked. Elizabeth appeared at Jessica's side. She must have been right behind her sister in the hallway. They really did get each other's backs.

Jessica's shoulders were slumped, and her lips were trembling. She almost looked . . . *scared.* Weird. *Maybe I'm overreacting,* Tia thought, feeling a twinge of guilt for coming down so hard on her friend.

"Jess, don't—"

"Trent didn't send you any of those things," Jessica blurted.

Tia blinked. Okay, that was *not* what she'd been expecting. "Then who—I mean, wait—how do you even *know* that?" Her ears were starting to burn, and her head felt like it was about to explode. "But you just told me you were helping him," she added, beyond confused.

"Actually, I sent them. Everything—the card, the roses, and the candygram," Jessica said quickly, her eyes darting around the hall, looking everywhere but directly at Tia.

Tia's jaw dropped, and her eyes narrowed. What was going on—and what was Jessica trying to prove?

"I know that it was wrong," Jessica rushed on before Tia could even respond. "But I thought that if I did it, you would realize that you wanted to be with Trent and you guys would get back together." Her voice grew softer as she finished speaking.

Tia knew that she should be furious. After all, she was upset enough when she thought that Jessica had helped Trent. This was ten times worse.

But instead of anger Tia felt defeated. A wave of disappointment came over her. She looked down at the worn tiled floor and blinked several times, wondering if she was going to cry. For a while Trent had tried so hard to get her back, but obviously he had finally given up. She didn't really have a valentine after all, even an unwanted one. Her valentine had been Jessica Wakefield!

This was one of the most pitiful and embarrassing things that had ever happened to Tia. She actually believed that Trent was going out on a huge limb when in fact he probably wasn't even thinking about her.

Jessica and Elizabeth both stood before her, their eyes wide and full of concern. Part of her was tempted to let them fuss and cheer her up, except that the other part was ready to kick Jessica into the next town over.

Tia stood up straighter. She couldn't let Jessica see that she had secretly wanted Trent to be the one sending her all of those things. She quickly replaced her disappointment with the anger she'd been feeling before. Why would Jessica pull something like this? What was she thinking?

Tia's eyes flashed. She was searching for just the right thing to say to Jessica—but her power of speech seemed to have temporarily left her.

The silence hung there for a moment until Elizabeth broke it.

"Tee, I know that Jessica was wrong here, but her heart was in the right place," she offered.

Tia still didn't know what to say. So many thoughts were racing through her head, and she felt like crying and screaming and being quiet all at the same time.

"I know I went about it the wrong way, like Liz said," Jessica admitted, nervously pulling a hand through her hair. She took a step toward Tia. "But is it really that big a deal? I mean, even though Trent didn't send you those things, he definitely wants you back. I was only trying to get you to realize . . ." She trailed off.

The hallway was beginning to fill as students

came out of the cafeteria and got ready for their next classes. There was no time to get to El Carro—not that she needed to anymore. Now that she knew Trent wasn't her secret admirer.

Tia, Elizabeth, and Jessica moved to the side of the hallway to let students pass by.

Tia wanted to walk away, but she was glued to the spot. She felt like a rug had just been pulled out from under her. Trent wasn't trying to get her back, and her best friends had made a fool out of her.

This Valentine's Day was turning out to be worse than she had thought it ever could be.

All he could do was wonder what they were arguing about in the hallway. They had been in deep conversation for a while now. And she seemed so upset. He wished he could just go over and put his arms around her and tell her that it was going to be okay. Whatever it was with her friends would pass.

Hopefully his note would cheer her up. He'd been working on it for a while, but he wanted it to be perfect before he gave it to her. To clearly express everything he'd been thinking.

He had always been a good writer, but his talent for stringing together words and sentences wasn't working for him with this letter. This was a really important note. He wished that he was better at saying what he felt. This had to knock her off her feet, convince her to meet him, and make her want to be his valentine.

The crowds in the hallway were beginning to build, and it was harder to see where they had moved.

Oh, well, he thought. *Now she'll only be more happy to get a note cheering her up.*

He took his books from his locker and smiled to himself. By this time tomorrow they might be a couple. If he didn't blow it tonight. If he thought of something half interesting to say in his note.

Couples floated by hand in hand, smiling. He had never thought he'd be this excited about Valentine's Day. It had always seemed like such a sappy, sentimental holiday. But if you really cared about someone, it wasn't that bad. It was pretty great, actually. And it was hopefully about to get better—after she got his note and they met face-to-face again. The bell rang, and everyone in the hallway scattered. He caught sight of the three of them going in different directions. He had to rush to get to class and figure out how to make his note better—and then get it to her before the end of the day.

"Phew." Maria let out a small sigh of relief, even though the bell had rung and she was late. By now Ken must have gotten the tickets, which meant they were even, and she could enjoy her flowers. Maybe this Valentine's Day could be saved. After all, she had a seriously amazing boyfriend who had gone out of his way to give her a great gift. She twirled the combination of her locker. Luckily her next class was study hall, and Mr. Shows never cared who was late.

Maria had opened the door to her locker, ready to grab her chem book and drop off her stuff from the morning classes, when she spotted something that hadn't been in her locker that morning.

Her breath caught in her chest. What was that?

Her hand trembled slightly as she reached for the small burgundy box with the white ribbon that was sitting on her locker's shelf. Only one other person in the world had the combination to her locker. And that box looked suspiciously like the ones at her favorite jewelry store in the mall.

Maria looked around the hall to see if Ken was standing there to surprise her. After all, the day was half over, and they hadn't even actually seen each other yet. She took the box from the shelf. Yes, it read *The Jeweler's Box* on it. Ken really was too much.

She opened the box quickly, her heart racing. She had never gotten jewelry from Ken before. It was even more romantic than the flowers. *And certainly more expensive,* she realized, cringing.

Maria snapped open the box and couldn't help but smile. Inside were the beautiful sterling-silver hoop earrings that she had admired the week before when she and Ken had been walking through the mall. They were gorgeous and totally expensive. If she remembered correctly, they were almost a hundred dollars. Ken didn't have that kind of cash. Between the flowers and the jewelry, he must have robbed a bank or won the lottery.

Before she knew what she was doing, Maria was holding the earrings up to her ears. Of course, she couldn't keep them. This was way too generous, but she could see how they looked in the small mirror she had inside her locker.

The delicate silver circles caught the light and shone. They really were perfect. Simple and classy. Just the kind of thing she wore. Why did Ken have to be so generous? Maybe she could tell him to return them? No, that would be way too mean. She had to give something else in return.

Maria slammed her locker door and took off down the hall, the box containing the earrings held tightly in her hand. She needed another idea—and fast.

"Jessica," Maria breathed as she saw Sweet Valley High's resident expert on boyfriend matters coming down the hallway. This was perfect. If anyone could help her think of the right gift for Ken it was Jessica Wakefield.

Jessica spotted Maria and gave a halfhearted wave. Maria noticed that she wasn't her usual giddy self. She hoped everything was okay because right now she required Jessica's undivided attention.

"Hey, Jess," Maria said. "How's it going?"

Maria could hardly wait to launch into her own dilemma, but she had to make sure there was nothing seriously wrong.

"Whatever," Jessica said, shrugging.

Not exactly the answer Maria was hoping for.

"Something with Jeremy?" Maria asked, secretly hoping she didn't open the floodgates.

Jessica brightened and stood a little taller. "No, everything with Jeremy is fine," she replied. "I got a bouquet of flowers from him today, and tonight we're going to see each other."

"Oh, that's good, then," Maria said, letting out a relieved breath. As long as things with Jeremy were fine, whatever was behind the sour attitude could wait. "Why aren't you in class?" she asked, confused.

"I have a pass," Jessica explained. "I figure I can be gone ten or fifteen minutes before Mr. Santoro sends out the guards. I couldn't sit still in economics today. So I'm just killing time."

"Great!" Maria nearly shouted. On any other day

Maria would have asked Jessica why she couldn't sit still in economics—it was obvious that she wanted to talk about it. But time was not on Maria's side. Emily Post would just have to forgive her. "I really need your help."

Maria pulled Jessica to the side of the hall in case any teachers poked their heads out of their doors.

"What's up?" Jessica asked. She frowned, tilting her head.

"You know how Ken and I agreed not to exchange gifts?"

Jessica nodded.

"Well, apparently I'm the only one who took the agreement seriously. Already today I've gotten a huge bouquet of flowers and some totally gorgeous earrings." She handed Jessica the box.

Jessica lifted the lid and gave a low whistle. "Wow," she said. She unscrewed one of the shiny hoops and took it off the velvet-covered backing to get a better look. "Ken has great taste."

"Great taste, a good memory, and no cash," Maria said. "I saw those with him last week in the mall, and I know that they were way more than he could afford. I already bought him some concert tickets off of John Maksel in second period. But I'm stumped for another gift."

"I'd be happy to help you think of something. I

like to help couples who actually want to be together," Jessica said, her tone unusually bitter.

Maria knew she couldn't let that one go. If she
wanted Jessica's help, she had to let her get whatever
was bothering her off her chest.

"What do you mean?" she asked, hoping it was
quick.

"I just tried to get Tia and Trent back together,
but it kind of blew up in my face. I'm not sure
whether Tia's even talking to me," Jessica explained.

Maria winced. "Ouch," she said. This Valentine's
Day wasn't going too smoothly for anyone, it
seemed—except all the nameless couples out there
who were practically on another planet, they were so
wrapped up in this holiday.

Jessica sighed and shrugged.

"Well." Maria smiled. "I have the perfect oppor-
tunity for you to make up your Valentine's Day
karma."

"Great, as long as I can get it done in the next five
minutes."

Maria let out a nervous giggle. They were working on a clock here. Not only was she dodging a possible detention for being this late, but Jessica had to
get back to class—and fast.

"I need an idea," Maria said. "What's the guy
equivalent to jewelry?"

Jessica looked stumped for a second, then seemed to focus on something over Maria's shoulder. A sly smile spread across her lips.

"Let's find out," she said, grabbing Maria's hand and leading her toward the pay phone near the door. There was a telephone book attached to a long chain.

Before Maria could even figure out what was going on, Jessica was flipping through the phone book.

"Hmmm, nothing like a phone book for a little inspiration," Jessica said.

"Jess, that's a great idea." Maria smiled.

Jessica looked down at her watch. "There has to be someone in here who can deliver something to Ken before the end of the day."

Maria bit her lip. There were only a few hours left in the school day, plus it was Valentine's Day. One of the busiest delivery days of the year.

"Cookies? A cake?" Jessica asked, flipping quickly through the book from back to front. She was so determined to help that she wasn't even looking anything up in the yellow pages, just paging through as fast as she could.

Maria shook her head. "No and no," she replied.

"Balloons?" Jessica said, looking up for Maria's reaction, her hand in place on the page advertising balloon bouquets and deliveries.

"Perfect!" Maria said. "No, seriously. The tickets were like the guy jewelry, and the balloons can be like Ken's flowers. Jessica, you are a genius!"

"Thanks. Glad to help!" Jessica gave Maria a quick hug. "I've gotta run, though. Let me know how it all works out."

She handed the book to Maria, open to the page for Sweet Valley Balloon Bouquets and Baskets.

Maria felt like a weight had been lifted from her shoulders. But she couldn't help but think how much this was going to set her back.

"I will," she promised Jessica as she punched in the number. "Thanks again, Jess!" she called out.

"No, thank you," Jessica responded.

"For what?"

"For bringing back my good Valentine's Day karma," Jessica joked.

Maria held her breath as she finished dialing. They had to make a last-minute delivery. They just had to. Maria drummed the receiver with her fingers as the phone rang once, twice. . . .

"Hello?" A frazzled-sounding woman answered the phone.

Maria bit her lip. This had to work.

"Hello? Is this Sweet Valley Balloon Bouquets?" she asked, gripping the phone tightly.

"Yes," the woman said. "Can I help you?"

"I hope so," Maria said. "Would it be possible to get a Valentine's Day bouquet delivered to Sweet Valley High before the end of the day?"

Maria held her breath as she waited for the woman's response. It sounded like she was instructing someone standing near the phone at the shop.

"No, not the get well—the best wishes," she said with an edge to her voice. "Hello?" she said, coming back on the line. "Well, it is late notice, and we're crazed over here. But I should be able to get something out within the next two hours."

"Great!" Maria said, exhaling loudly.

She gave the woman her emergencies-only credit-card number and Ken's name before hanging up. Her parents had to understand why she needed to use the card they'd given her. After all, this was the biggest emergency she'd had in a while.

Maria was so relieved. She had never thought such a low-key holiday could be so much work. A romantic, inexpensive dinner on the beach seemed like a distant memory, a plan that they had made years ago. And forgotten.

Maria Slater

How to Make Back All the Money
I've Spent on Ken Today

1. Baby-sit the awful Snyder twins every weekend for the rest of the school year
2. Sell my old doll collection (packed up in boxes somewhere in the attic)
3. Beg Mom and Dad
4. Sell a vital organ

Dear Valentine,

I've been waiting for so long to tell you how I feel, and now I can't find the right words. You are the most amazing girl I've ever known, and no one else has ever measured up. Maybe our relationship is in the past, but I hope it can still have a future too.

It's still coming out wrong. So why don't you let me say it in person?

Meet me at First and Ten tonight at 6 P.M. I'll be carrying a red rose.

CHAPTER 7

First and Ten at Six

Just a couple more classes to go, Jade thought as she left her English class. This day was dragging even more now—ever since her lunch with Evan. It was like he had turned into the antiboyfriend overnight. Would he be back to normal tomorrow?

And was it really so much to ask that her boyfriend treat her well on the most important day of the romantic calendar—give her a card or something? It didn't even have to be store-bought—homemade would do just fine. And really, what was the point of finally being in a good relationship that had made it past the fifteen-minute mark if there was no recognition of Valentine's Day to show for it?

Jade straightened her backpack and flipped her dark hair over her shoulder. She looked down the hall at the sea of happy faces coming toward her. Ugh. Was *everyone* happy today? Was she the only one with this problem? All of the boyfriends of the girls she knew were bending over backward trying to impress them. Flowers, cards, candy, jewelry.

Frustrated, Jade turned in the other direction and nearly ran smack into Annie Whitman. Annie was, of course, carrying a big bouquet of flowers. Twelve long-stem roses, to be exact. They smelled amazing, and Jade couldn't help but inhale a large breath of the flowers' scent before looking away.

"Hi, Jade!" Annie said brightly. Annie was always in a good mood, even before she had started dating George Hill. But now she constantly had a smile on her face. Just the type of person Jade did *not* want to see right now.

Annie's cheeks were flushed, and Jade was sure hers were a sallow yellow in comparison.

"Hi, Annie," she said back with about as much enthusiasm as she could muster. "Are those from George?"

"Yes," Annie said, moving the glass vase to her other hip. "He just gave them to me."

Jade nodded. Was there any escape? She looked down the hall for a familiar face, someone else she knew, someone not quite as perky as Annie. But there was no one, only happy Annie.

"So, any Valentine's plans?" Annie asked Jade.

Jade cringed, wondering how to handle the question without ending up on the receiving end of some major pity. But before Jade could even open her mouth, Annie was already talking about the plans she and George had for the night.

"I've been working on a poem for George. I finally got it just right and had it framed last week. I wrote it in calligraphy. I hope he likes it. If not, I also got him a gift certificate to the sporting-goods store that just opened near the mall."

"That sounds great," Jade said automatically, nodding as if what Annie said really interested her. All she wanted to do was scream.

"I'm making him dinner tonight at my parents', and I know he burned a CD for me, so we'll probably listen to that," she finished with a sigh.

Jade blinked, trying to seem interested.

"I'm so glad I ran into you," Annie continued. "All of my other friends are single, and I feel kind of funny making a fuss over my Valentine's Day plans. But I knew that you would understand. Isn't it fun?"

Jade nodded and smiled, gritting her teeth. She felt like she was in some kind of bad teen movie where the cool girl was flaunting her popularity in the nerd's face.

"So, are you excited about your plans? What are you and Evan doing?" Annie asked expectantly.

There was no way Jade could admit how lame her Valentine's Day was turning out to be.

101

"It's a surprise," Jade blurted out, immediately kicking herself. All that would accomplish was getting Annie even *more* interested.

"That's so exciting!"Annie squealed, right on cue. "You can tell me, though, right?"

"Nope, no one knows." Jade shook her head. *Including me,* she thought.

"Wow, sounds romantic. And a lot more exciting than the old dinner-and-CD routine," Annie said.

Yeah, well, life on Fantasy Island generally is.

"Will you tell me about it tomorrow, then?" Annie asked. "I've gotta get to class."

"Yeah, sure," Jade replied. Great. Now she had to come up with some elaborate lie by tomorrow. And she'd very likely burst into tears midstory too.

"Happy Valentine's Day," Annie called out as she started down the hall.

"You too," Jade answered.

Tomorrow she'd just have to tell Annie that the big plans had fallen through. Then she'd feel like even more of a loser. As soon as Annie was out of sight, Jade's eyes welled up with tears. She bent down and got a drink of water from the fountain. *I'm not going to cry. I'm not going to cry,* she told herself.

"Happy Valentine's Day," someone shouted to a friend across the hall.

Jade was so sick of Valentine's Day. She just

wanted to run out of her red-and-pink-decorated school and never come back. She didn't want to think about it or talk about it anymore. Not with a boyfriend who didn't seem to care about it—or her.

Ken couldn't believe that he was sitting in his last class of the day and he hadn't seen Maria yet. Where could she have been hiding? At least he had managed to get to the mall and buy those earrings. Never mind the fact that he had totally wiped out the savings account his dad had urged him to start before going away to college. He'd probably be able to earn it back this summer. He hoped. He also hoped Maria liked the earrings, considering what he had paid. Tomorrow they probably would have been on sale, marked down for the post-Valentine's sales. Oh, well, it was worth it—it was Maria. Ken smiled and squirmed in his seat.

Tonight was going to be great. He was sure to get a big kiss for his present, and Maria would probably wear something red. She looked great in red, and she knew he loved her in that color. Plus the beach was his favorite place to go with her. They could walk along the shore, eat good food, kiss some more.

Ken was snapped out of his daydreaming by a

knock on the door to the classroom. He glanced up and saw it was an aide from the front office.

"I have a delivery for a Ken Matthews," the aide announced. "Is he here?"

Ken frowned. Weird. He had never gotten a delivery before in school.

"Yeah, that's me," he said, sitting up a little straighter.

Just then the aide whipped a bouquet of balloons inside the classroom.

The whole classroom started buzzing. Some kids in the front were actually laughing.

It was a little strange, but what was so funny about . . .

Then Ken caught sight of the message on one of the balloons. *It's a Girl!* it read. The bouquet was entirely done in pink and white and was clearly meant for new parents—not him.

The aide looked a little confused, standing in front of the classroom with a bunch of balloons that were congratulating a new arrival.

Ken felt his face grow warm. He knew it was bright red. Even his ears burned.

"Well, Ken, are you going to come up and get your delivery?" Mr. Reinsel asked, an eyebrow raised.

"Um, there must be some kind of mistake," Ken said, rising to his feet. He wiped his damp hands on his jeans.

"Why, Matthews? Was it a boy?" he heard one of the guys on the team who sat near him say in a loud whisper.

The entire class erupted into laughter. Even Mr. Reinsel looked amused.

Ken walked up to the aide and took the bouquet back to his seat. What on earth was this, and why had it been delivered to him?

Fortunately Ken sat in the last row, so he tied the balloons to his seat and sat down. There was a card dangling from the ribbons. He untied the envelope and read the card. *Happy Valentine's Day! Love, Maria.*

There was definitely a mix-up here. The card was right, Ken was sure, but they'd obviously attached the wrong bouquet.

In front of him Mr. Reinsel was back to talking to the class. Ken was glad that the focus was off him now. That had to be one of the most embarrassing things that had ever happened to him.

He looked up at the balloons and smiled. The thought was nice even if the balloons were wrong. But now Maria had given him two gifts to his one for her. Great! He was behind again.

He scrunched down in his seat and sighed. This Valentine's Day was breaking him.

* * *

Elizabeth headed to her locker after her last class, relieved to be done at SVH. She just wanted to put the day behind her and go home. Between not having a boyfriend and getting caught in the middle of Jessica and Tia's fight over Trent, she'd had about as much as she could stand of this holiday.

Why did Jessica have to stick her nose in their business? she wondered as she opened her locker. But before she could give it more thought, something caught her attention out of the corner of her eye—a piece of paper floating to the ground. She leaned forward to pick it up, and as she opened the folded paper, her eyes grew wider. *I've been waiting for so long to tell you how I feel, and now I can't find the right words.* Was this for her? Yes, her name was there at the top. Who was it from? The note said that he and Elizabeth had a past and a future. . . .

She tried to continue reading, but the excitement was making her feel light-headed and a little dizzy. As the letters started to blur, she reminded herself to keep breathing—*Inhale through the nose, exhale through the mouth.* This little trick she picked up from a yoga tape she once rented really did the job.

Meet me at First and Ten tonight at 6 P.M. I'll be carrying a red rose. She had to reread that line three times before it sank in. The idea that someone would go out on a limb like this for her was so crazy.

Does this mean I have a secret admirer? she wondered. *Couldn't be,* she reasoned. Fairy-tale plot twists weren't written into the Elizabeth Wakefield life story. She looked over the letter again, slower this time so that she could decipher any hidden meaning. *Been waiting all year to tell you how I feel . . . Meet me . . . tonight at 6.* No hidden meaning there.

I guess I have myself a real secret admirer, she affirmed. But she couldn't stay with that feeling for long. What if it wasn't real? What if it was just a prank, like the whole Trent-Tia-Jessica thing? What if she showed up at First and Ten and no one was there—or worse, a group of her friends was waiting around to get a good laugh or possibly some tape for *America's Most Embarrassing Home Videos*?

Too many thoughts were swirling around in Elizabeth's head. She took another deep breath and tried to pull herself together. There was nothing to lose by going. Besides, most of her friends had more important things to do on Valentine's Day than play a trick on her. And if they didn't, they were probably looking forward to heading straight home for their own private pity parties.

Then again . . . what if the note came from someone she didn't want to deal with? It did mention that they had been together in the past, but when Elizabeth went through all her exes, she couldn't think of one who was available who she'd want to go out with again. How would she be able to mask her disappointment? How would she get out of it without hurting his feelings? *I'm supposed to be putting myself first now,* Elizabeth reminded herself. *And taking chances—not letting opportunities pass by.* It was all part of the new life plan she'd put into action this semester. She would just have to be willing to take a risk. She needed to go and see who wrote this amazing note. Now there was just one problem—how on earth would she manage to stay in her skin until six o'clock rolled around?

Jade threw her backpack across the living room onto the couch. She couldn't remember when she'd last been this depressed. Evan had let Valentine's Day come and go without doing absolutely anything for Jade. Not even a heartfelt hug and a happy Valentine's kiss.

"Jade, honey. Is that you?" her mom's voice rang from the kitchen.

Jade looked up, surprised. Her mom was never home when she got back from school. Ms. Wu worked long hours to support them, and even though she'd cut back a little since she got sick in the fall, she still came home later than Jade usually.

108

"Yeah, Mom. What are you doing home?" Jade asked, walking through the doorway and into the sunny yellow-and-white kitchen.

"Mr. Hendrickson actually decided to not be such a spoilsport on Valentine's Day and let everyone leave a little early," Ms. Wu replied. She gave Jade a bright smile, the kind of smile Jade had been wishing for from Evan all day, then went back to loading the breakfast dishes into the dishwasher.

"Cool," Jade said, trying to sound enthusiastic. She pulled up a wooden stool and sat down, resting her chin in her palms.

You know you're in trouble when your mom's Scrooge-like boss has more Valentine's Day spirit than your own boyfriend, Jade noted. Her mom's boss was usually asking everyone to stay late for no extra pay, not letting them leave early.

"Uh-oh," her mom said, turning her attention away from the dishes and facing Jade. "What's wrong? Does it have something to do with the fact that you're not out with Evan right now?"

Jade nodded, and her eyes filled with tears for about the hundredth time that day.

Only this time, in the privacy of her own home, she actually let the tears fall.

"Jade, are you okay?" Ms. Wu was by Jade's side

in an instant, her voice full of concern. She rubbed Jade's back and handed her a tissue.

Jade couldn't speak for a second, only shake her head.

"Evan didn't." Jade's voice cracked.

"Evan didn't what?" Ms. Wu asked.

"Evan didn't even wish me a happy Valentine's Day," she said, looking up at her mother for a reaction.

Ms. Wu put her arm on her daughter's shoulder before she pulled up another stool and sat down.

"Other girls got huge bouquets and presents and at the very least a card," Jade explained. "I know that Evan has never been into celebrating the 'commercial' holidays, but I was hoping it was all talk—like how he doesn't eat junk food but really does. Turns out, he really doesn't celebrate Valentine's Day. At least not when he's with me."

Ms. Wu leaned over toward Jade and tilted her head. "Are you *sure* it's not all talk? Maybe he just needs you to make the first mention of it," she suggested.

Jade shook her head. "No, he really doesn't want to celebrate Valentine's Day."

Her mom was sweet to try to convince her otherwise, but she hadn't been there to see Evan all day. He was definitely ignoring the holiday on purpose.

"This reminds me of a story about you, Jade," her mom said, walking over to the sink to fill a glass of water for Jade.

At least Jade had managed to stop bawling, but there were still tearstains on her cheeks.

Ms. Wu handed Jade the glass of water and sat back down on the stool. "Do you remember when you were five and found out there was no Easter Bunny?"

Jade shook her head again and blew her nose. She couldn't imagine where her mom was going with this.

"Well, you asked your father and me not to have Easter baskets because it was all a lie. But then when you woke up on Easter morning and thought you had no basket, you were crushed," her mom reminisced. "Of course, you did your best to pretend it didn't matter, but we caught you crying in your bedroom when you thought we were downstairs."

Jade chuckled, despite how upset she was. That did sound like her, she had to admit. She hadn't changed much—even in all these years.

"Sorry," she apologized to her mom sheepishly. "Guess I was hard to please even back then."

Ms. Wu shook her head. "You weren't a difficult child—you just wanted an Easter basket like any

111

other kid. Easter Bunny or not. But you were too stubborn to admit it," she added with a smile.

Jade took her face out of her hands and looked at her mom. Sometimes she had really good stories that made sense. And she could give really wise advice.

"I gave you your basket, and you were thrilled," Ms. Wu said. "Do you see what I'm saying?"

Jade nodded and sat up straighter on her stool. She did get it, and her mom was right. Deep down, most people wanted to be a part of things, which sometimes meant celebrating certain holidays even when they claimed not to believe in them. Jade had done it, and Evan might be doing that right now, but it was kind of hard to know.

"Evan's so upset, though, he really may not feel like celebrating anything," Jade began.

"That's right. Evan is upset. And he has every right to be. He's going through a very difficult time," Ms. Wu offered. "So maybe now's the time for you to do something special for him. Besides, where is it written that the girl has to wait around for the boy to initiate the Valentine's Day festivities?"

Jade nodded slowly and looked at her mother. She could be right about this. It sounded true. Jade could definitely see Evan blowing it off when deep down he did want to celebrate with her. He might even feel like it was wrong for him to enjoy a holiday for couples if his parents weren't happy anymore. But if Jade was the one to get things going, then Evan wouldn't have to feel guilty.

Her mom was right. She just needed to make the first move.

Alanna Feldman

Conner,

Happy first Valentine's Day! Who'd have thought we'd make it this far? (Just kidding.) I can't tell you how happy I am that we're together. I know there'll be more, but this one is special—just like you.

Thanks for helping me turn my life around. Can't wait to see you tonight.

XXXX
OOOO
Alanna

Conner McDermott

Hey, Alanna,
   Have a good one—

                    Conner

CHAPTER
FROM ANOTHER GALAXY

8

As Tia headed for the parking lot, she kicked at a stray candy heart all the way from the school's entrance to her car. This had to be the most depressing day of her life. First she had thought that the only valentine she got was from a guy who had really wished he was with Jessica. Then she found out that the valentine wasn't even from him, but from Jessica.

The worst part was that she actually felt let down when she found out Trent wasn't the one sending her all of those things. It had been kind of cool to think that even though she'd told him that they weren't getting back together many times before, he cared enough to keep trying.

Tia grabbed her keys out of her bag and put them in the door lock.

"Tia! Tee!"

Tia whipped around and saw Jessica running toward her. Great. Jessica was probably the last person

Tia wanted to see right now, but she couldn't exactly ignore her.

"Tia, I am sooo sorry," Jessica said earnestly when she reached her. She bit her lip nervously. "I've felt so bad since lunch. I don't know what I was thinking, playing your secret admirer. I mean, you've made it more than clear that you don't want Trent back. I just should've butted out." Jessica tucked a stray blond hair from her ponytail behind her ear.

Tia leaned against her car door. It was nice that Jessica had run after her. And she did have *I'm sorry* written all over her face.

Still, Jessica needed to know exactly why Tia was angry. She seemed to be missing the most important point. This wasn't about Trent—this was about her and Jessica.

"Jess, the reason I got so angry is that I don't think you considered *my* feelings in all of this," Tia started.

Jessica crinkled her brows. "But I did it all for you. I wanted to help you and Trent get back together," she protested.

"Actually, I think you did it for you," Tia said, with a little reluctance. It might sound harsh, but Jessica had to face the truth.

Jessica's face turned bright red, and her jaw

dropped. "How could you say that?" she asked in disbelief.

Tia cringed, but she needed to get this out. "I'm not trying to be mean, but I think you wanted to get me and Trent back together so that you wouldn't feel guilty about his trying to kiss you."

"Well, of course I felt guilty about that, but that's not the only reason I did it," Jessica argued. "The main reason was because I know how badly Trent wants you back, and I think you two belong together. I was just trying to speed this along."

Tia paused, wondering if maybe she *was* being too hard on Jessica. She really did seem sincere. But that wasn't the point. "Did you ever think about what would have happened if you hadn't gotten to me in time?" Tia demanded. "What if I had gone all the way over to Big Mesa and told Trent to stop trying to get back together with me? He would have looked at me like I was from another galaxy. Can you imagine how humiliating that would have been?"

Jessica's face scrunched up into an expression of guilt. "Ouch," she admitted. "I'm sorry, Tee—I guess I just didn't think that far ahead. I just thought it was a good way to get you to realize that you do want him back."

Tia stiffened, feeling her face flush. Fine, so

maybe Jessica's stupid plan had accomplished what she wanted it to. But what good was it knowing that she still wanted him if he wasn't even trying to get her back anymore?

"I was right, wasn't I?" Jessica pressed, her confidence already returning as she saw the way Tia reacted. "You *were* happy to get all that stuff from Trent. You do want him back, don't you?"

Tia sighed. "Jess, I think it's time to leave it alone," she warned. "I know you meant well, okay? I'll cancel the contract on your life. But don't you have a date to get ready for?"

"Only if I have your forgiveness," Jessica said.

"Of course you do," Tia said. "Now get outta here." She gave Jessica a friendly push, and they both laughed.

"Okay, I'm leaving," Jessica promised. "But just *think* about what you were feeling before, when you thought all those gifts were from Trent."

Tia narrowed her eyes at Jessica, and she obviously got the message because she rolled her eyes, then headed off across the parking lot.

At least one of us has a fun date tonight, Tia thought as she got into her car. The parking lot was now nearly empty. Everyone had left in a rush to get ready for their dates.

Tia started the car and let the engine idle for a

minute. All of a sudden she didn't feel like going home just yet. She needed to drown her sorrows in a double mochaccino. House of Java was on the way. She could crawl into a booth and be alone for a while.

Guess it really is my first official Valentine's Day alone, Tia thought. Too bad there was no convincing herself that she was okay with that anymore.

Will had read the same sentence three times but kept losing his place on the computer screen. He had been at the *Tribune* for an hour already, but he just couldn't concentrate.

Normally he would have been psyched by anything Mr. Matthews gave him to do. He felt alive when he walked through the door, ready to take on any challenge thrown his way. Today he was even being allowed to write the conclusion to a piece on the Sweet Valley University girls' volleyball team, but Will's heart wasn't in it. He was just too disappointed with what had happened earlier that day.

At first he had expected Melissa to say that she was just kidding about not being able to make it tonight, but she was serious. She had chosen her family over Will. She'd given him the brush-off so casually, like it was some minor thing. His stomach still got tied up in knots when he pictured her walking away, as if it was just another date on just another day. She knew that he had been planning this for weeks.

Sometimes he had to wonder why he even bothered. Melissa could be so heartless.

Will shook his head, then continued to bang away on the keys, not even paying much attention to the letters and words that appeared before him.

Erika poked her head out over the cubicle next door. "Everything okay?" she asked, smiling. "You're typing pretty fast and furious over there. Were you inspired?"

"Not really," Will said, hardly looking up.

"But tonight's the big night. Aren't you psyched?" Erika asked, coming around into Will's cubicle.

Will swallowed hard before swiveling around in his chair to face Erika. After all, she had helped him plan this night too. He kind of felt like he almost was letting her down, even though it wasn't nearly as bad as what Melissa had done to him.

"Melissa canceled," Will said flatly, trying not to show how upset he really was. "She backed out because of some family thing," he added, unable to keep his voice from cracking.

Great, now Erika would think he was some kind of wuss.

Erika moved closer to him and put her hand on his arm. Her face was a mixture of surprise and sympathy. Will noticed how her hand made the rest of his body feel warm. With her standing this close, Will smelled the faint, citrusy scent of Erika's perfume. He looked up at her, and their eyes locked. She had on a tight, cropped pink sweater set and gray pants. She looked and smelled fantastic. But most of all, she seemed really concerned about how Will felt right now.

"How could she cancel a Valentine's date with you?" Erika said softly. "She's crazy."

Will took a deep breath. If he didn't know better, he'd think that Erika Brooks was hitting on him. But that was impossible.

"She'll regret it," Erika said, taking her hand from Will's arm and hopping onto his desk. Her dark red boots began swinging back and forth underneath. "I know lots of guys. And you are definitely not the kind girls cancel on."

Will held his head up a little higher as he listened to Erika's compliments. She was making him feel better—a lot better.

"Really?" he managed to get out.

"Oh, totally. Melissa's insane not to appreciate a guy like you."

As she hopped off Will's desk, he caught a

glimpse of her flat, tan stomach. Matt and Josh were right. Erika was hot.

Plus she was being so nice. Totally cool.

"Well, she seems to care more about some uncle she never sees and hardly knows," Will said.

Erika shook her head and pouted.

"I've been around so many big-headed older guys, I'd love to be with someone who cared so much and went out of his way like you did to set up this date," Erika said. She was now leaning against the cubicle wall, flashing that same piece of stomach that Will was trying hard not to look at.

Will shook his head. "It was no big deal, really," he said modestly.

"Hey, you two."

Will looked up and saw Mr. Matthews standing next to Erika.

"Any Valentine's plans?" he asked them.

There was a long pause. "No," Will finally answered. "My girlfriend couldn't do anything tonight." God, they must both think he was such a loser.

"I've got nothing to do either," Erika said, shrugging. "No valentine."

Will could have sworn that she quickly looked at him when she said that. Could she have wanted him to know that she didn't have a boyfriend?

"Oh, I'm sorry," Mr. Matthews said with a sheepish

grin. "I thought that maybe you two were spending Valentine's Day together."

Erika giggled, and Will felt a warm blush creep up his neck.

Mr. Matthews was usually pretty perceptive about the things that went on around him. After all, he was a reporter—he was always sniffing for a story. How had he been so off on this one?

"Well, I was wrong. Happy Valentine's Day anyway!" he said, then walked away.

There was an awkward silence after Mr. Matthews left. Will chuckled nervously.

"Well, he was all wrong," he said, looking at Erika for reassurance.

"Was he?" she asked, moving toward Will. "I mean, you are here on Valentine's night and not with your girlfriend."

Will wanted to respond, but he was speechless. Erika was definitely flirting with him. He couldn't believe it. She had been so unattainable in high school—so above him. Girls like Erika hadn't flirted with him since he had been scoring touchdowns on the football field. He had to admit it felt good.

Plus knowing Erika would be willing to spend Valentine's night with him was a total ego boost—especially since Melissa wouldn't.

*   *   *

"I'll get it, Mom!" Andy shouted as he jogged down the stairs and over to the front door. "This better be Evan because he's about the only person I can deal with right now," he mumbled under his breath. Looking forward to playing pool this evening was all that had gotten him through the pain of this day, which against all odds had actually gone *downhill* since lunch. He'd accidentally parked in a teacher parking spot and gotten a written warning from security. He'd also gotten a C on his history quiz, after he'd vowed to start taking that class more seriously. All of that would have sucked on any day. But after what happened with Dave? Andy shook his head, as if he could shake the thoughts of Dave out of it somehow.

The doorbell rang again, and Andy reached out and yanked open the door, relieved when he saw who it was.

"Hey!" Evan said. "I brought chips and dip. Bring on the challenge!" He held up a container of salsa and some corn chips, then stepped inside the house.

Andy felt better already. Watching Evan treat the challenge like a major sports event was entertaining enough to take his mind off the day's events for a while, at least.

"Thanks," Andy said. "I'll grab some sodas, and we'll head to the basement." He closed the door.

"Let the games begin," Evan said. He threw his arm into the air over his head.

"Wow, someone is really pumped up for this," Andy said with a grin.

"Yeah, well, anything is better than Valentine's Day," Evan said. "Besides, I've been waiting all day to blow off steam on your pool table."

"It has been a pretty lame day," Andy said, walking toward the kitchen. Evan followed. Andy opened the refrigerator door and grabbed a six-pack of sodas.

"Well, that all ends now," Evan said. "At least for me. I'm gonna wipe the floor with you, man." He gave Andy's shoulder a light punch.

Andy laughed. This had definitely been the right idea for tonight. Hanging out with Evan made Andy feel better—normal.

He opened the door to the basement and flipped on the light switch. The pool table was in the middle of the basement, and the dartboard was on the far wall. There was also a backgammon, chess, and checkerboard in one corner and a table set up for poker in another. It was the perfect place to hang out, especially when you didn't want to talk to anyone else. Andy, Conner, and Evan had spent many rainy Saturdays in this basement.

Andy couldn't believe that next year they'd all be in college and not able to get together like this. *No more depressing thoughts tonight,* Andy reminded himself. This was the time to relax and unwind.

He put down the sodas, and Evan opened the chips and salsa. They stood there, silent for a few minutes, shoveling food and drink in their faces. Andy hadn't eaten much for lunch, and he was starving now. At least he had his appetite back—that was a good sign. The sick feeling in his stomach had passed.

"I'll rack," Evan said. His mouth was full of chips, but he was already grabbing the balls from each pocket of the pool table.

Andy wiped his hands on the sides of his jeans before taking a cue and rubbing chalk on the tip.

Yep, this was where he was supposed to be. Dave was just a memory.

"You wanna break?" Evan asked.

Andy nodded and crouched, poised to hit the cue ball, when the doorbell rang again.

"Who could that be?" Evan asked.

Andy put down his cue, puzzled. It couldn't be Conner. There was no way he'd miss his date with Alanna. But who else could it be? Conner was probably just stopping by for a quick round. Andy went upstairs to see, taking the stairs two at a time.

"Be right back!" he shouted.

"Right behind you," Evan said. "Gotta check out the competition."

Andy opened the door. "Yo, Con—" He stopped short as all the air seemed to whoosh out of him at once.

127

Standing there on Andy's front step was Dave, his hands stuffed awkwardly in his front jeans pockets. Dave. Here, at Andy's house.

"Uh, hi," Dave said nervously.

Andy was too stunned to speak. He felt his heart squeeze inside his chest, and then it started beating more rapidly. What was he doing here? Why had he shown up after what had happened in the park today?

Andy slowed down his breathing, reminding himself why he and Dave couldn't be together. He just couldn't be with a guy who wouldn't admit that he was gay, not after Andy had worked so hard at getting over his own shame.

Finally he managed a hello in return to Dave.

"Were you expecting someone else?" Dave asked, looking right at Andy.

He seemed to see right through him, Andy thought with a shiver.

"Uh, no. Well, sort of. We thought our friend Conner might be stopping by."

Dave peered around Andy, noticing Evan behind him. He definitely seemed to tense up, even though Andy wouldn't have thought it was possible a second ago.

"Hey, Evan," Dave said softly.

Evan nodded. "Hi, Dave." He put down his soda can on the entryway table, then glanced back and forth between Andy and Dave. "Actually, I just remembered that I've gotta go," he added. "I forgot about that calc assignment tonight. Better bolt. You guys have—um, have a good night, okay?"

He gave Andy an awkward clap on the shoulder, nodded again at Dave, then shot out the door, leaving Andy alone with Dave. Obviously that's what Evan thought Dave wanted. But should Andy even agree to talk to Dave? That was the real question. He had to make up his mind, though. He tugged on his hair and shifted his weight to the other foot, thinking about what he should say. He opened his mouth, and the words popped out.

"Do you want to come in?" he asked, opening the door wider.

Had that been a mistake? Did he really want to talk to Dave right now? Too late.

Dave was already inside, nodding and looking relieved that Andy hadn't turned him away.

Andy didn't know what to do next. Dave was standing in the middle of the foyer, looking around like he had no idea what to say. But he'd better come up with something because Andy was pretty sure he'd used up the last of *his* current vocabulary.

Jade Wu

Possible Valentine's Day Gifts for Evan

1. A dartboard (not very romantic, but something he'd like)
2. A reconciliation for his parents (not at all possible in the real world but something he'd love)
3. A book on how to be a more thoughtful boyfriend

Ken cut the engine on the car and checked his watch again. He knew he was early to pick up Maria. A whole hour early, to be exact, but he needed to see her—the sooner, the better.

He wanted to apologize for misunderstanding their Valentine's Day agreement. Clearly he had missed something. Plus Maria had been way more generous in her gift giving than Ken had been in his. Even if she had embarrassed him with the It's a Girl balloon bouquet. His face still turned red just thinking about having to take that pink-and-white thing from the office aide and parade it through the classroom.

The truth was that despite how stressed out this day had made him, he was also touched by Maria's thoughtfulness. She really was amazing, even if she was breaking the bank in the process.

He probably should have called first to let her know that he was early. Too late now. He opened the car door and looked up at the sky. Clouds had been forming all afternoon, and he hoped that it didn't rain on their beach picnic. Sweet Valley was normally the sunniest place on earth. Ken sighed and ran a hand through his thick blond hair.

He was about to walk toward Maria's door when he realized he'd forgotten something. He opened the passenger-side door and picked up the bouquet of tulips and sunflowers he'd picked up at the florist on the way. This would make up for that last gift he'd received. Ken hoped he was wearing the right thing. He had on a green button-down shirt and his nicest khaki pants. It was amazing how he still cared about what he wore when he saw Maria, even though they'd been together for so long.

He rang the bell at the Slaters' front door and heard footsteps. He quickly put the bouquet behind his back. Maria opened the door, and her mouth dropped. She looked up at the clock in the hallway and furrowed her brow.

"Ken! Hi. Did I get the time wrong?" she asked with a puzzled frown.

"No, I'm early. I should've called," he replied. He walked inside, keeping his back to the door so that Maria couldn't see the bouquet behind him.

"I wanted to get here early to thank you for all

the gifts you gave me today. They were so great. I can't wait to go to the concert."

Maria beamed. "I wanted to thank you . . . ," she started as Ken whipped out the flowers from behind his back.

"Ta da!" he said proudly. "Happy Valentine's Day!"

Maria's forehead wrinkled in confusion, but she smiled and took the bouquet.

"Ken, you've been so generous. The earrings and two bouquets of flowers? It's too much, really."

Now it was Ken's turn to look confused. What was she talking about? *Two* bouquets?

"Two bouquets?" he repeated out loud.

"Yeah, one from this morning and now this one," Maria said. She cocked her head, studying him closely. "Did you already forget or something?" she asked.

Okay, Maria got flowers this morning, he thought, still trying to process everything. *But they weren't from me.* Was someone else sending Maria flowers? But why wouldn't the jerk have told her he wasn't Ken? It didn't make any sense.

Ken shook his head slightly, taking a deep breath. "Um, I didn't send you flowers this morning," he confessed.

"What?" Maria said. She put the bouquet down on the table in the hallway. "That's so strange. They

133

were on my desk in homeroom," she continued. "I was the envy of everyone in there—especially Lisa Weiss. . . ." She trailed off.

"Maybe they were delivered to the wrong room or put on the wrong desk," Ken said, thinking out loud, trying to come up with a logical explanation.

Maria nodded slowly. "Yeah, that could have happened, I guess. If that's what happened, some poor guy is probably wondering why his girlfriend never thanked him for the flowers."

They were silent for a few seconds, trying to think of what could have possibly happened.

Of course, Ken thought. Maria sat next to Lisa Weiss, and Ken was friends with Lisa's boyfriend, Chris Wolsch. Chris had put the flowers on Lisa's desk that morning. *I know that much.*

"That's it. Did you by any chance sit in Lisa Weiss's seat this morning?" Ken asked.

"No," Maria replied. "Why?"

"Well, because Chris Wolsch left her some flowers, but he told me during gym that she didn't even mention it to him. In fact, she gave him the cold shoulder all day. He was wondering if flowers weren't good enough or something." Ken shrugged.

Maria's smile gave way to laughter. "Chris must've left the flowers on the wrong desk," she explained. "He's actually done that before—left Lisa notes on my desk. I don't know why I never thought of that. Lisa even saw the bouquet and said that she wished he'd given her flowers."

Ken started laughing too. "They're probably finding out right now about the mix-up."

"So, wait. You kept to the bargain and didn't send me the flowers," Maria said. "But I thought I had blown it, so I bought you those concert tickets this morning from John Maksel."

"You did?" Ken said. He was touched that Maria had wanted to give him something right away. She'd done a great job at picking the perfect gift. The Friction rocked! But she must have spent a fortune. John wouldn't have sold them to her cheap, he was sure.

Maria nodded. "I was confused, so I started sending you gifts. I guess now the balloons were a little over the top, but once I got the earrings, I felt like I needed to get you something else. Did they deliver those to you?"

"Yeah, they did. With an It's a Girl! message on them. I figured that was a mix-up." Ken chuckled.

"What It's a Girl message?" she asked, another look of confusion clouding her face.

"They sent me a balloon bouquet of baby congratulations to my last class," he explained.

"Oh my God, Ken! That's so embarrassing. I'm sorry!" Maria said, grabbing his arm and laughing. "You must have been ready to crawl under your desk," she added.

Ken shrugged. They looked at each other, silent for a minute, then burst out laughing again. Suddenly it just seemed so funny. They had been running around all day trying to match and outdo each other when in fact, the whole thing had been started with an honest mistake.

Ken couldn't wait to see Chris and Lisa and let them know about the trouble they had started.

"Sorry to interrupt, you two," Mrs. Slater said as she walked into the hallway. "Looks like you're having fun. What's so funny?"

Maria shook her head. "Just a huge misunderstanding, Mom," she explained, winking at Ken. "What's up?"

"Well, I just got a call from Sweet Valley Balloon Bouquets. They wanted to apologize about the delivery mix-up and offer you a free bouquet to send anywhere," she said, reading from her notepad. "Apparently some new parents got a Happy Valentine's bouquet and you got theirs."

"Actually, Ken got it!" Maria started laughing again. "In his last class today."

Mrs. Slater chuckled. "Oh, that's what was so funny."

"Part of it, yeah," Ken said. He thought about trying to give the whole story but decided to spare Mrs. Slater the details.

"I still can't believe I never thought that they could have been on the wrong desk," Maria said. "I'm so sorry, Ken."

"No, I'm glad it worked out this way. It gave me an excuse to give you the presents you deserve," Ken replied.

"Well, I trust you two understand what's going on because frankly, I'm completely lost," Mrs. Slater said. "Guess I've been out of high school for too long." She smiled and walked upstairs.

They burst into laughter again. Ken couldn't get over how crazy this was. All the confusion, all the money spent trying not to spend too much. Two hundred and fifty dollars, he estimated. That was some serious cash.

Suddenly it sank in. Yeah, that *was* some serious cash. Ken stopped laughing. He looked at Maria. "We both spent a lot of money today trying to outdo each other. Are you mad?"

Maria stared back into his eyes. "Not at all," she said. She stepped toward him and folded into his arms, giving Ken the same warm sensation he always got with Maria close to him. He breathed in her perfume and the fresh scent of her shampoo. This frantic day had all been worth it.

"Happy Valentine's Day, Maria," he whispered in her ear.

"Happy Valentine's Day, Ken," she whispered back.

Why is he here—what does he want to say? Andy wondered for what felt like the millionth time in the past five seconds, if that was at all possible. His heart was racing. He needed to do something. He needed a plan—he was just so surprised to see Dave at his door that he didn't know what to do.

"So, do you want something to drink?" Andy asked. That was lame, but his mom would have said it was the polite thing to do. "We've got sodas in the basement." He felt like he was babbling even though all he did was ask one simple question.

Dave shook his head no, and there was another pause.

"Could we talk somewhere private?" Dave asked, looking intently at Andy.

"Uh, yeah. Sure," Andy said. He took a left toward the family room, and Dave followed. The family room was less formal than the living room, and Andy needed all the comfort he could get from his surroundings right now. His stomach was doing flip-flops again. He wished he hadn't wolfed down those chips in the basement.

Andy sat down on the tan couch while Dave took a seat in an overstuffed chair. He didn't sit back into it, however. Instead he sat on the edge, his body bent forward and his hands clasped together.

Andy purposely sat back on the couch. He didn't want to appear as nervous as he felt. He wanted to ease the tension by speaking again, but he'd used up anything he had left to say when he made the beverage offer. So he waited for Dave to talk.

"First, I wanted to apologize about the park earlier today," Dave said, looking down at his hands and then up at Andy. "You were right. I did know those kids. They go to my school, and I just got really freaked out about being there, out in the open, with someone I care about."

At least he's apologizing, Andy thought. He realized that he had been wrong, which was a good start. *And he said he cares about me,* Andy realized, with the accompanying increased heart rate. But Andy reminded himself not to jump to any conclusions. Nothing had changed. Right?

"But that's not the real reason I'm here," Dave said, finally sitting back a little bit in the chair and unclasping his hands.

What other reason could there be? Andy wondered. After what happened in the park, he wasn't sure what else was left to say between them.

"See, my dad asked me this afternoon if I had a hot date for Valentine's Day," Dave explained. He paused, studying Andy's face for a reaction. Andy was determined not to give him one. He sat there on the couch as expressionless as possible while his mind raced.

"I told him no, that I had recently lost the person I wanted to be with," Dave continued.

Andy's breathing quickened. He couldn't believe Dave said that—but he probably hadn't told his dad that *person* just so happened to be a guy.

"Anyway, as I said it, all I could do was think about how I had felt earlier in the park today. I realized how important you were to me and how I had to do whatever I could to make things work between us."

Dave had zoomed through the last part of his speech, and it took a few seconds for Andy's brain to catch up with the words. He cleared his throat and sat up a little straighter as he struggled to process everything. He wanted to let Dave know that he had his attention.

"My dad is picking up Evan's mom right across the street tonight. And I'm over here despite the fact that he might see me—or my car," Dave finished.

Oh my God, he told his dad, Andy thought. He started to smile, but Dave saw it and winced.

"I know what you're thinking, and no, my dad doesn't know that I'm gay—yet," Dave said.

Andy should have known that it was too good to be true.

"But I'm telling him this weekend—no lie," Dave said quickly, sinking back into the chair. "It's worth it for me to tell him now that I've finally found someone I want to be with. I owe us both that."

This time Andy let a big, slow grin spread across his lips. Dave had finally realized what he needed to do, and he knew when he was going to do it. That was definite progress. There was hope for Dave. *Yes!*

Dave smiled too, and Andy felt like they were both finally on exactly the same page.

"So does this—um, are you happy?" Dave asked. "I am, but I'm also nervous," he said before Andy could respond.

Andy nodded. "Yeah, I'm—I mean, of *course* I'm happy. It's amazing. And it's really cool that I was the one who helped you feel like you could—you know, do this."

"Well, it took me long enough," Dave said with a sigh.

"Don't be so hard on yourself—it's a big deal." As Andy said it, he remembered how much he'd agonized about telling *his* parents. But they had been great. And Andy was sure Dave's dad would be too. "Are you sure you want to do this?" he couldn't help asking. He had to double-check, even though the only answer he could stand to hear was "yes."

Dave nodded. "Positive. I have to do it for me."

That was the right answer, Andy thought. This was mostly for Dave.

"Listen, I can talk you through it," Andy volunteered. "We can act the whole thing out. I'll play your dad."

"Sounds like fun," Dave said sarcastically as he rolled his eyes. "You'd have to shave all that gorgeous red hair to get into character, though. But hey, it's for a worthy cause."

Andy laughed. Secretly, he was thinking that it *would* almost be worth it. Not that he'd ever admit that to Dave. Bald just wasn't his best look.

Maybe this Valentine's stuff wasn't as bad as Andy had thought it was. What a difference a day had made in their relationship. Things were definitely looking up.

"How 'bout that soda?" Dave suggested.

Andy nodded. "No problem," he said. They headed down to the basement to grab the sodas.

Yes, this could be the best Valentine's Day ever.

Evan picked up the TV remote from the coffee table and flipped the channel. His night was officially a disaster. But he was happy for Andy. Hopefully Dave showing up there tonight meant that there was a chance for the two of them. That would be cool.

Too bad it meant Evan was stuck here with the big, empty house. Although moping was something that was definitely best accomplished alone.

He was probably the only one by himself on Valentine's Day. He actually felt a little pang as he thought that. He didn't think that the holiday spirit had caught him, but maybe he was as prone to it as everyone else. Suddenly he thought about Jade and couldn't help cringing. He hoped he hadn't disappointed her, but the great thing about Jade was that she seemed to understand why Evan didn't go for all that silly, sentimental stuff. Anyway, there was nothing he could do now—the day was almost over.

At least he had a pizza to look forward to. He had ordered his favorite tofu-and-veggie health pizza and was expecting the delivery at any minute.

He switched the channel again, searching for a good movie to go with his pizza. But everything he landed on seemed to be a love story. He couldn't stomach any of that. Where was the dumb-guy action flick? That was what he needed right now. Something mindless and full of bad one-liners to mock.

Evan padded to his mom's bedroom to check out her video collection—not that he expected to find anything but chick flicks there. Just as he was resigning himself to watching a documentary on the life of Johann Sebastian Bach, he heard the doorbell ring.

Must be the pizza guy, the only other poor soul alone on Valentine's Day, he thought as he headed for the front door.

He swung open the door, already reaching into his back pocket to grab his wallet. But when he saw who was standing there, he froze.

"Happy Valentine's Day!" Jade said cheerfully. "I come bearing treats." She lifted a brown-paper shopping bag toward him. He caught the name Cornucopia—his favorite health-food store—on the front.

"Jade, hi. I mean, Happy Valentine's Day!" he said. He couldn't believe how happy he was to see her. Her smile made him go embarrassingly gooey inside. But then he felt a stab of guilt—ignoring Valentine's Day while the rest of the school was in full-on celebration mode must have been tougher on her than he realized. But here she was, at his front door, with a bag full of stuff for him anyway.

"Can I set this all out in the kitchen?" she asked, holding up the bag.

"Sure," he replied, taking the heavy bag from her and leading the way.

He wasn't sure what to say next. An apology for being a big scrooge? But she didn't *seem* mad.

"I hope you don't mind that I just came over without calling," Jade said. He recognized that nervous glint in her soft black eyes and felt like a supreme jerk. How could he have made his own girlfriend afraid to celebrate Valentine's Day with him? And here she was, as cheerful as someone whose boyfriend had spent the entire day showering her with gifts and flowers.

"No, I'm glad you're here," he said, feeling strangely shy.

Jade smiled, then turned and emptied the bag, placing the packages on the counter. Evan's heart caught in his throat. She had gotten him eco-friendly carob treats, protein bars, and ginseng-carrot-tomato-seaweed smoothies for two. And what had he gotten her? Nothing.

Evan was about to tell Jade how amazing she was to have done all of this. But before he could even open his mouth, she cut him off.

"Evan, I'm sorry if you didn't want to celebrate Valentine's Day. But it felt weird not being with you tonight."

Evan started to speak, but Jade wasn't done.

"I know you're going through a really hard time with your parents' divorce. But I'm here for you, and just because things didn't work out for them, it doesn't mean that all love is bad or has to end."

A slow smile started to form on Evan's lips. Jade was so adorable when she got all passionate about something, and she had obviously thought so hard about this. How lucky was he? He couldn't believe she'd showed up here. How many girls would have after how he'd acted today? This might be the best surprise he'd ever received.

"Anyway," Jade went on. "I thought that no matter what, we should celebrate Valentine's Day together. Yeah, it's cheesy, I know, but we *are* a couple." She paused, then gestured at the snacks on the counter. "I brought you all of your favorites. I don't think I forgot anything." She bit her lip, then met Evan's gaze for the first time. "Okay, so what are you thinking?" she asked.

Evan just stared back at her, unable to think of how to respond. Jade was absolutely right, about everything. But what she *hadn't* said was that he'd really messed up big time today.

Jade's smile faded, and her eyes filled with disappointment. She started grabbing the stuff off the counter and piling it back into the bag. "I'm sorry, I shouldn't have—"

Evan moved toward her and grabbed her, pulling her close to him. "It's perfect," he murmured into her hair. He carefully pulled the carob bars out of her hands and placed them back on the counter behind them. "*You're* perfect." And before she could say another word, he pressed his lips to hers, wondering how he ever could have thought he'd rather be anywhere but here, with Jade, tonight.

Ken Matthews

Dear Maria,

I'm so happy that we're together for Valentine's Day. I know this will be the best one ever because I've realized that with or without gifts, I love being with you. You make me happier than anyone else ever could. Happy Valentine's Day!

Love,

Ken

CHAPTER 10
A Double Blow

Will kicked at the carpet in his cubicle and stared at the clock overhead. For weeks he'd been planning this night, but it wasn't turning out to be anything like he'd expected. He had finished up his assignment from Mr. Matthews, even though it hadn't been easy to concentrate. Thoughts of both Melissa and Erika had been playing out in his head constantly.

Did Erika want him? If so, what was he supposed to do? Well, he was *supposed* to resist. He had a girlfriend. *Yeah, a girlfriend who doesn't exactly put me very high on her list of priorities.* Meanwhile Erika was making it more and more obvious that she was into him. It felt good, he had to admit. Very good.

He pushed his chair back from his keyboard and stretched his arms overhead.

Erika must have heard his sigh or his back crack because she popped her head up over the partition that separated their cubes. They'd been doing that all afternoon—talking and flirting, going back and forth.

"Are you finished?" she asked.

Will nodded and swallowed—hard. She really was beautiful. And she wanted to be a journalist too. Plus she liked sports. Could she be more perfect?

"First stop, Sweet Valley, next stop, the big offices of *Sports Illustrated* in New York," she said with a laugh.

"Hey, how did you know I want to work there?" Will asked playfully.

"It's easy to spot the ones who have ambition to get out of Sweet Valley." She walked around to Will's cube and perched herself on the edge of his desk again.

She was sitting closer to him than usual, swinging her long legs back and forth underneath the desk.

"I mean, don't get me wrong, it was a great place to grow up and all, but I'll be ready to leave when the time is right," she said, looking intently at Will.

Will nodded. He totally agreed with her. He tried to stammer out a response but felt like his tongue was stuck to the roof of his mouth. He'd talked to Erika before and been totally relaxed. What was so different now? Something had changed today. Even though she was only a couple of years older, the conversations Will had with Erika were nothing like the ones he had with Melissa. He felt older, more respected around Erika.

Stop it, he told himself, the words leaking into his mind as an instinct, a reflex. He couldn't think about another girl like that. But why not? Just how long had it taken Melissa to throw herself at Ken when Will was lying at home in bed, not even able to *walk?*

He blinked, realizing Erika was still waiting for him to reply. "I've always planned to be out of Sweet Valley in four years," he told her, somehow managing to form the words. "In fact, my deadline is August fifteenth."

"August fifteenth—that's my birthday!" Erika exclaimed, swinging her legs back down on the floor.

"Mine too. That's the day I'll be twenty-one," he replied. *Wow, that is weird.* They even had the same birthday.

Erika grabbed his arm. "Amazing! I never met anyone with the same birthday as me before. Have you?"

Will shook his head. Again he was mute. Erika pulled her hand away, but it had lingered there for a few seconds longer than a casual touch. He was sure of that. He also knew that if he didn't get out of the office at that moment, something might

151

happen between them. And the worst part was, he wasn't so sure that was a problem.

"Are you leaving soon?" she asked, as if guessing his thoughts.

Will nodded reluctantly.

"I have a few more e-mails to read," she said. "Wait and I'll walk out with you."

"Okay," Will said. He swiped his palm across his forehead after Erika disappeared around the corner. The offices were air-conditioned, but small beads of sweat had formed around his hairline. Erika Brooks definitely made him nervous.

He stood up and grabbed his bag, shoved in a few piles of paper he needed, and glanced at his watch.

Right now Melissa was probably sitting down to dinner with her family. On top of everything else, Melissa hadn't even given him a card or anything. It was as if Valentine's Day hadn't really arrived yet. After everything that they had been through this year, he at least deserved that much. A night alone with his girlfriend to celebrate—if he could call her a girlfriend. What kind of girlfriend wouldn't convince her parents to let her spend Valentine's Day with her boyfriend?

Will grabbed a stack of papers and moved them to his out bin.

Despite all of the distractions, he'd actually gotten a lot done that day. This internship was turning out to be a great thing. For more than one reason.

He checked his e-mail one more time to see if Mr. Matthews wanted anything else before Will left for the night. He had to admit, he also hoped that Melissa had sent him an e-mail apologizing or at least wishing him a happy V-day.

No such luck. His mailbox was empty. Will shut down his computer.

His stomach was reminding him of the good dinner he was missing out on. It gave a low rumble.

Maybe Erika would want to grab a quick bite, some pizza or something? Will thought. After all, he hadn't called his parents to tell them about Melissa canceling, so they weren't expecting him for dinner. Maybe they wanted to be alone or had made their own plans for the night already—like everyone else who was part of a couple.

Erika walked by Will's cube with a stack of copies of the *Tribune*.

"Ugh, I'm going to have newsprint all over me," she joked.

Will laughed. "I bet it'd look good on you," he said, feeling like an idiot as soon as the words were out. But Erika didn't seem to mind at all. She barely responded, as if she was used to hearing things like that all the time. Which she probably was.

"So, almost ready to leave?" Erika asked. "I'm just going to put these papers back in Mr. Matthews's office."

Will followed her into his boss's office, waiting in the doorway. "Actually," he began as casually as he could. "I was thinking of grabbing something to eat first. My parents aren't expecting me at home, and I'm starving anyway. Do you, uh, want to come with me?" He hoped he hadn't just made a big mistake. What if Erika had just been acting so nice and flirty because she felt sorry for him? Maybe she wouldn't want to go.

But Erika was already nodding. "Sure, I know some places near SVU. That's great."

Will grinned. "Just let me finish packing up and we'll head out."

"What are you in the mood for? I could go for some pizza," Erika said.

That was weird. Will had been craving pizza ever since Melissa canceled on him.

"That was just what I was thinking," he said.

"Great!" Erika said enthusiastically. A few of her papers fell from under her arm to the floor. She put the rest of the stack down on the floor and reached for them. Will rushed over to help her.

As he bent down to help Erika pick them up, their eyes locked for what seemed like the hundredth time. But this was different. Will was close enough to see that her blue eyes had these amazing flecks of gold around the pupils. He swallowed hard but couldn't move.

The next thing he knew, Erika had closed her eyes and was leaning toward him. Will felt her warm lips on his, and he held his breath, not believing what was happening. Erika Brooks was actually kissing him. His entire body was numb.

Erika broke away and got to her feet. Will followed, still feeling the pressure of her lips on his. Then he realized that was because Erika was kissing him again.

He wanted to pull away. He knew that this was wrong, but it was somehow right. Will's arms encircled Erika's waist. He couldn't believe that he was doing this—he couldn't believe that he was kissing her back.

Tia had been at House of Java for hours. At first she had just meant to have one mochaccino. Then she got started on some homework, and before she knew it, it was almost dinnertime! She was fully caffeinated and only hoped that she'd be able to fall asleep later that night and forget that this day had ever happened.

She got into her car and started the engine, letting it idle for a few minutes before pulling out of the HOJ lot.

At least Valentine's Day was nearly over. That was a huge relief. She turned up the volume on her radio. There had been a ton of couples strolling in and out of HOJ, and she'd done her best to avoid having to look at them. At least tomorrow things would be back to normal and she could put Trent out of her mind once and for all. He really was harder to shake than she had thought he'd be. But he wasn't trying to get her back. She had to remember that important fact.

Home at last, she thought as she pulled into her driveway. It was starting to get a little dark, and the clouds overhead looked like they might open up anytime. Tia hardly even looked up at her house as she reached for her house keys. She lifted her leg and balanced her bag on her thigh, searching for her key ring. It had to be in there somewhere. She had to remember to put her house keys on the same ring as the ones for the car.

She found it buried in the bag and looked up at her front door. She stopped—shocked.

"Oh!" She breathed in sharply, then lost the fight of balancing her bag on her leg, and it dropped on the ground.

But her eyes never left the walkway leading to her house. There, in the twilight, sitting on a bench, waiting for her, was Trent. Behind him was the front porch, all decked out in Valentine's Day decorations. There were red and white balloons and pink streamers. And Trent held a bouquet of flowers in his hands.

Is this a joke? she wondered. But she knew it couldn't be. She quickly picked up her bag and walked toward the house, still not sure if what she was seeing was real.

As she got close to the door, Trent stood up awkwardly. He'd probably been sitting there for a while. God, Trent showing up on her doorstep on Valentine's Day was more romantic than anything Tia could have even imagined.

"Hi," Trent started. "I hope it's okay that I'm here. Your mom and dad know. They even had me in for a snack. Your mom got such a kick out of watching me decorate, she got out her camera and started taking pictures."

Tia nodded and smiled. That sounded just like something her mom would do. She saw Trent's shoulders relax. He must have been really nervous waiting there for her.

"I'm glad that you're not angry," he said. "Listen, I know that you told me you needed your space and

157

not to push things, but it's Valentine's Day, and you're all I could think about. I had to do this. I know it's kind of goofy. . . ."

Tia shook her head. "Actually, I think it's sweet," she said softly.

Trent broke into a wide grin. *That was all he needed to hear,* Tia thought. That he hadn't been wrong to keep trying with her.

"So were you thinking about me?" Trent moved toward her, and she took in the way his red pullover sweater and dark blue jeans accented his toned, muscular build. Had she forgotten how gorgeous this guy was? Or how warm his eyes were when they looked at her?

No, and that's why Jessica really got to me today, she realized. She wasn't even close to being over Trent, but she *was* finally ready to forgive him. How could she not when he'd done all of this?

Right then, all Tia cared about was when the stupid guy would kiss her already. As if reading her mind, Trent stepped closer to her, and then it was happening—they were kissing. Tia closed her eyes and melted into his arms, feeling better than she had in a long time.

Elizabeth put her foot down on the gas. She had just a few minutes to get to First and Ten before six. She had rushed home in a total daze from her late-day surprise and then found herself drawn into a seemingly endless debate with Jessica over who this guy could be. Finally Jessica had taken off for her *own* date, so Elizabeth was free to go on hers.

Elizabeth couldn't wait to meet this mystery guy. She and Jessica had read the note over and over and even taken a quick look through last year's yearbook. They just couldn't figure out who would make sense. But that only made her more excited and anxious to see who he was. They had a past. Hmmm . . .

That could be a good or bad thing. Elizabeth wasn't exactly having a good guy year. Maybe—hopefully—her luck was about to change.

Elizabeth turned into the First and Ten parking lot and grabbed the first available spot. She checked her watch. One minute after six. She wasn't sure if that was "fashionably late," but she really couldn't wait any longer to see who he was.

She glanced in her rearview mirror to make sure she didn't have any lipstick on her teeth. Getting ready had been another ordeal. Jessica had insisted that she borrow one of her shirts, a burgundy wrap top, and then Elizabeth had finished with her favorite black pants and her new strappy sandals. Elizabeth ran a finger through her hair and smiled at her reflection, satisfied that she was ready. This was it. Time to meet her secret admirer.

She opened the door to the restaurant and was greeted with the irresistible smell of french fries and onion rings wafting through the air. As good as it smelled and as hungry as she was, she couldn't even think about eating.

Elizabeth scanned the restaurant. She saw a few couples and a bunch of families with little kids, but no guys who were alone. She walked toward the back of the restaurant, her eyes darting across the red leather booths.

They were all occupied or empty. No one looked like they were waiting for anyone. Was he not here yet? Did he even exist? Maybe it was a joke after all. Her stomach clenched, and she felt like she was about to be sick. If this was a practical joke, it was so not funny.

She walked quickly back to the other side of the restaurant, suddenly feeling self-conscious and exposed. It was like everyone there was watching her, secretly laughing at her. She started to blush and even felt tears come to her eyes. She was a fool. No one wanted her.

"Elizabeth! Liz!" a deep voice called out from behind her.

Elizabeth turned around in the direction of the

guy's voice. Her breath caught in her throat when she saw him. Not him. She hadn't even thought of *him*. But there he stood, holding a single red rose and looking even better than she remembered. Looking incredible, actually. "*You're* my secret admirer?" she asked. Then she broke into a huge smile.

Melissa walked through the front doors of the *Tribune*. It was a nice building, even for a small, hometown newspaper. Now she could finally see where Will had been spending nearly all his time after school. But she hadn't expected to feel this nervous about being there. Excited, yes, but not nervous. It was just Will. They had been together for years. Still, this was the first time that she had surprised him with something like this. She actually had butterflies in her stomach just standing in the building's lobby.

The lie would be worth it to see the look on his face when she walked in the door. Just a few minutes after six. Perfect timing! She had worried that she'd be a little late because she had to wrap Will's gift—a new greatest-hits CD from his favorite band. She also had dinner reservations for seven P.M. If she got up there fast, they might even be able to squeeze in a walk on the beach beforehand since the restaurant was near the ocean.

She smiled to herself as she approached the receptionist's desk. No one was there, but on the wall was a list of offices and where each department was.

Melissa found the sports department and punched three on the elevator button nearby. The newspaper occupied more than one floor! Pretty impressive. It was a much bigger and nicer office than she'd imagined too.

What would Will say when he saw her? She was sure that whatever happened, she'd have a great story to tell her friends tomorrow. One that would top everyone else's.

Melissa got off on the third floor and looked to her left and right. She thought the map had instructed her to go to the right, so she followed the long hallway to the end.

She knew that Will and the other sports intern shared a cubicled office next to Mr. Matthews's office. So when she saw a nameplate at the end of the hall with Mr. Matthews's name on it, she looked to both sides. On one side was the ladies' room and on the other, an office.

The door was partly ajar, so she didn't bother knocking. Besides, her plan was to shout, "Surprise!" to Will and have him run into her arms and give her a great big hug. She'd been envisioning the moment all day.

Melissa began to push open the door. Then she stopped—horrified. She stood there staring, her jaw hanging open.

Was what she was seeing real? It couldn't be. This was more than she could handle.

Melissa stepped back and almost fell over. She felt like she was watching a movie. Like all of this was happening to someone else.

How could Will—*her* Will—be standing there kissing another girl? As Melissa watched in horror, they pulled apart slightly, and Melissa got a glimpse of the girl's face.

She blinked, unable to believe she was really seeing this. What . . . It couldn't possibly be *her*. No way. There was no way that Will—her *boyfriend*, Will— was in the middle of kissing Erika Brooks.

WILL SIMMONS
6:05 P.M.

Mmmm. No, I shouldn't be doing th——mmmm.

MELISSA FOX

6:05 P.M.

Turn around, Will. Come on, do it. I want to know exactly what you have to say when you see me standing here. And it had better be good.

ELIZABETH WAKEFIELD
6:12 P.M.

I never thought Valentine's Day could be this perfect. To think, after all this time the greatest guy was right under my nose. And now we have a second chance.